# Gill Harvey

Piccadilly Press • London

First published in Great Britain in 2005
by Piccadilly Press Ltd,
5 Castle Road, London NW1 8PR
www.piccadillypress.co.uk

A catalogue record for this book is available from the British Library

ISBN: 1 85340 812 3 (trade paperback)
EAN: 9781853408120

1 3 5 7 9 10 8 6 4 2

Printed and bound in Great Britain by Bookmarque Ltd.
Text design by Textype Typesetters, Cambridge
Cover illustration by Susan Hellard
Set in Stempel Garamond and Papyrus

*For Ahmed*

# Chapter One

I remember looking out of the plane window and thinking, *Wow. Desert.* Nothing but yellow emptiness, broken up with ridges, rocks and a few more rocks. But then the plane dipped and banked, and I saw this strip of emerald green, so bright and lush it seemed unreal, with a shimmering strand of water running through the middle of it. And the thought passed through my mind that the people who lived in this strange sandwich of green and yellow must be pretty special, one way or another.

Stepping out of the plane was something else. *Whoosh.* The heat hit us like a bathful of hand-hot water. Except that it was bone dry, and the air smelt of dust.

'It's gone four in the afternoon, Jen,' muttered Marianne, fanning herself with a magazine as we were herded across the tarmac and on to a bus, like sheep. 'How can it still be this *hot*?'

'Welcome to Egypt, Mar,' I said. I looked at Karen and grinned. We'd expected this – not the heat, because we'd had no idea it would be this hot either – but Marianne moaning. She's tough to please, is Marianne, but we love her for it when she digs her heels in and gets us what we want. Half the time, we can't be bothered to kick up a fuss about anything; we know we can rely on Marianne to do it for us.

'I'll die if it's like this all the time,' she declared.

'There might be a complaints desk in the terminal,' I said. 'Maybe they could do something about it.'

'Very funny,' she replied, frowning at the bloke who was squashed up next to her. He was a little on the large side, and had already broken into a sweat.

The bus roared into life and dumped us at the terminal. Luxor airport: destination sun and freedom! I'd finished my A-levels, just turned eighteen and I was off on an adventure with three of my best mates. Well, as much of an adventure as a Saturday job and a year's savings could pay for, which was only a fortnight's package holiday. But that was good enough for us – me, Karen, Izzy and Marianne. We were all in the same boat, that July. When we got back to the UK, we'd have a few short weeks together before the grand parting of the ways and a whole new life at uni.

Maybe it was this that made Luxor seem so full of promise, but I reckon it was more than that. Already, I could feel that this place was unlike anywhere else I'd ever been. You think, when you go on a package deal, that everywhere's going to be pretty much the same; that's how it seems when you go with your parents, anyway. But this was definitely different somehow. Even in the airport, there was this buzz in the air – the air-con working overtime, guys in long blue or white gowns jabbering in Arabic into mobile phones, that constant smell of sweet dust and the wail of Arabic music playing in the background somewhere. Out we went to the tour operator's minibus, and we soon realised we were the only teenage girls in sight. There weren't any fit guys either, just a bunch of lager louts mixed in with the families and the blue rinse brigade.

The air-con was blasting, but all the same the minibus was stifling. We were driven along roads clogged with all kinds of traffic – decrepit white taxis, donkeys overloaded with fodder and spanking new tour buses. I stared at it all, catching sight of palm trees waving above what looked like half-finished houses, the struts still sticking out of the top, painted in muddy pastel shades. I spotted some kids playing football in the dust and realised they were barefoot. This was a different world.

Then Marianne pulled a packet of Wet Wipes from her bag and handed them around, mopping her forehead dramatically. 'We should have gone to a Greek island,' she announced. 'Too hot. Too much dust. No fit guys.'

I giggled. We could always rely on Marianne to provide us with a pithy put-down, whatever the situation, and Luxor was no exception. 'You've only just arrived. Give it a chance,' I said.

Marianne sniffed. 'You would say that. This was your idea, Jen.'

Her green eyes glowered at me, and I grinned, thinking she was kidding. Of course it was my idea. I was almost always the one who suggested doing stuff and no one ever complained about it much. Not even Marianne.

But there was a silence and Izzy looked a bit anxious. 'Come off it, Mar,' she said. 'We all agreed to this.'

I looked at Izzy in surprise. Was there really an issue here?

'Yeah,' agreed Karen. She gave Mar a playful prod with her sandal. 'Anyway, since when did *you* check out guys on holiday?' It was a well-known fact that Marianne had spent all her previous holidays being dragged around European cities by her parents, who insisted on taking her to shows and restaurants every evening.

Karen's words hit the spot. Marianne looked embarrassed – a rare event. But then we all watched as she smoothed down her straight black hair, a slow grin spreading across her face. 'Never had the chance before. Maybe now's the time.' She glanced around the minibus. 'There's got to be more than *this* at the hotel.'

Was this the Marianne we knew and loved? Ice Queen Mar, who was still allergic to guys and got away with it because she had the sharpest tongue in Surrey? She prided herself on being far too cool for messy boy stuff. So of course, this was the last thing I'd ever expected her to say. I was going to remember it later, though.

Ten minutes later, we seemed to have reached the centre of town, and stopped outside the Horizon hotel. In we went, pairing off to find our twin rooms. I was sharing with Karen, of course. We were best mates and had known each other since we were eight. We'd stuck together through changing schools, first boyfriends, first bras – the lot. And while I was always pushing the boundaries and trying out new stuff, she just stuck by me, looking pretty and innocent in a girl-next-door sort of way, which somehow managed to keep us out of trouble. I owed her a lot.

We'd got to know Marianne and Izzy later on – Year Nine or thereabouts. They had been the aloof pair in our class. They managed to make their school uniforms look weird and arty with edgy accessories and outlandish hairstyles, and it seemed like they looked down their noses at everyone. And then I'd seen this showdown between Mar and a stupid, bullying prefect where Mar had made her look like the piece of snot she was. I respected her after that and tried to be more friendly. To my surprise, she was friendly back, and Izzy joined in.

Izzy was a lot less outspoken, though. Despite her wacky appearance, she was a bit of a whizz at maths and wanted to be an economist. She was lanky, boyish and fiercely loyal to Mar. We soon worked out that she was secretly quite studious and liked nothing better than a quiet life; funnily enough, that was exactly what Mar provided, because no one dared mess with her. What's more, I soon realised that Mar's cutting tongue was really funny as long as you weren't on the wrong end of it and if she really laid into someone, you knew sure as hell that they deserved it. Before long, the four of us had become inseparable.

Karen and I plonked our stuff on our hotel beds and explored the room. This was the normal bit, the bit you'd expect. It could have been anywhere, no amazing view, nothing 'Egyptian', just a plain twin room with an en-suite loo and shower. We went down to the lobby and fifteen minutes later got the drill from the tour guide, an Egyptian man named Mohammed, who spoke enthusiastic English. There was a whole range of trips we could go on – to the Valley of the Kings, the mortuary temples, the temple of Karnak or a boat trip up the river. As he waffled on, I saw he had his eye on us – probably thinking about what four eighteen-year-old girls, let loose in Luxor, could get up to. He came over and personally recommended that we go on the guided trip to Karnak the next day. Then he raised a knowing eyebrow and said we might be interested in the disco at the Hathor hotel that evening. 'Good for young people,' he said. 'Belly-dancing. Free entry for residents of the Horizon.'

It sounded OK, despite the eyebrow. So we decided to go.

I'm blonde, and let's face it, blondes get used to being looked at. But this 'disco' was something else. We might as well have had two heads each, judging by the effect we had when we walked in. There were gaggles of Egyptian guys hanging out around the walls, all dressed in tight jeans and with one eye on the door to check out the talent. They all seemed to spot us at once. There were hardly any other tourists. The lager louts were there, ploughing through beers in a corner, and there were a few other huddles dotted about. We must have stood out a mile.

We made a bee-line for the bar and tried not to catch anyone's eye. Not that it made any difference. They were soon all around us like flies, only harder to swat away.

'Hey, you very beautiful. You dance with me?'

I shook my head. A guy in bright white jeans thrust his hips forward and leaned in closer.

'Where you from? You no like Egyptian man?'

*Spare me the subtlety*, I thought. I risked a quick glance at his face and wasn't impressed. His hair was slicked back like some bad Elvis joke and his face was one big leer.

He grinned. 'Why you no talk? This not good way. I show you how Egyptian dance.'

'No thanks,' I said, peering round him for the others. They were all up to their necks too. Marianne's face was like thunder. I skirted round Elvis and led the way, head held high, to a table right in the corner. The others took my cue and followed.

'Pervs,' announced Karen, the minute we all sat down.

'Gross,' added Izzy, nodding.

Marianne was tight-lipped. 'That guy tried to grope me,' she said darkly, nodding in the direction of the men. 'And we've only just arrived.'

She looked at me accusingly, and I got the feeling that she really *was* mad at me for bringing us to Egypt. Mar had always reserved her withering looks for people outside the group before, but now all of a sudden I was getting them too.

I took a deep breath. 'OK,' I said, smiling brightly. 'No more hotel discos. But we might as well check out the belly dancer, now we're here.'

We got more drinks and kept the pervs at bay with looks like daggers until the dancer came on. She took over a quarter of the room, dancing in this skimpy, tatty sequined costume with holes in it and heavy make-up. I've only seen belly dancing on the telly before, but I wouldn't have recognised it. She hardly seemed to know what she was doing and just wobbled about, blowing kisses at all those guys. God, they loved it.

Then we saw that another group of Western girls had pitched up and were knocking back drinks in the far corner. They were a bit older than us, and were dressed like tarts – skirts up to their armpits. We'd only just arrived and hadn't fully figured out the dress culture yet, but at least we'd had the sense to cover up a bit more. The Egyptian guys didn't seem offended though. They'd piled right in there.

I felt a nudge from Karen. 'Look,' she said.

I looked. There was a girl wearing a bright pink ra-ra skirt that rode up her thighs and a top that looked about three sizes too small. I stared. She was snogging Elvis.

We didn't see what happened next. We got up and out of there and high-tailed it back to the Horizon in one of those decrepit white taxis. We were in too much of a hurry to negotiate a fare before we got in and talk about a rip-off! It cost us a total fortune, but we were way too fazed to react.

Things seemed to be on the up after breakfast the next day, when we went out on to the hotel terrace and saw the view over the Nile. It was gorgeous – palm trees dotted around, the morning sun glinting on the water, pinky-yellow mountains rising up in the distance on the other side of the river. It felt like waking up on a film set. On the downside, it was only eight-thirty a.m. and already sweltering.

The others seemed in a pretty good mood, thankfully, and while we polished off our coffee I decided there was nothing for it – we just had to go for it. This was our first hard-earned holiday together so I wasn't going to waste it moaning about the heat, whatever Marianne might say. So I took on my usual role of geeing the others into action.

'Come on, girls,' I said. 'We've got a date with a few Egyptian gods. Let's bag the back of the tour bus to Karnak.'

But we were too late. The lager louts had got there before us. We spent the mercifully short journey to Karnak sandwiched between a family of three squalling kids whose parents had a very limited vocabulary, and a group of women who all looked about sixty and were obviously mad about ancient Egyptian ruins. It was difficult to know what to listen to – 'Shurrup! Just shut it, right!' or 'Last time I was here I decided to study the era of Seti I – you know, the mortuary temple and so forth as well as his marvellous contributions to Karnak . . .' We rolled our eyes. Marianne got her Wet Wipes out and mopped.

The bus ground to a halt and we clambered out as fast as we could to escape our lovely companions. But in seconds, we were surrounded by swarms of Egyptian kids instead, all trying to sell us stuff – miniature pyramids, alabaster cats, bits of papyrus covered in hieroglyphs and God knows what else. We gawped at them in panic until Mohammed came to the rescue and shooed them off. He ushered us past them and in through the gates with a flourish and we heaved a sigh of relief.

So this was Karnak. Its massive, yellow limestone walls towered over us, all covered in carvings and hieroglyphs. I hadn't exactly been swotting up, but I knew it was one of the biggest temples, and I could vaguely remember a few things about the Egyptian gods from doing Ancient Egypt in Year Five. That was about it. But Mohammed was clearly a man on a mission. He had this gleam in his eyes as though he was about to rip the veil of ignorance from our eyes and reveal the world's greatest treasure. Maybe that's how he saw it.

It wasn't quite like that for us. The temperature seemed to have notched up another ten degrees since we'd left the hotel. The rest of the group had closed in on us too, and it was all too obvious that someone's Soft and Gentle roll-on wasn't working. We started shuffling from one gate to another, or pylon, as Mohammed insisted on calling them. God, he could drone for Egypt, he really could, even over the noise of the squabbling kids – though to be honest I would have listened a bit more if I hadn't been aware of Izzy and Marianne feeling so miserable. Karen will put up with anything and even she looked wilted. The big area with all the pillars – the Hypostyle Hall – was a bit cooler and we managed to escape Mohammed's monotone to prop ourselves up against some pillars in a corner.

'This sucks,' said Marianne in a matter-of-fact tone.

The rest of us were silent. I could just hear Mohammed's voice – '. . . the great king Ramesses II followed in Seti's footsteps and defeated the Hittites in the Battle of Kadesh, as shown in these reliefs. Here, you see that he claimed it was a great victory but in fact we know that the Hittites claimed the same . . .'

I spotted the lager louts a few pillars away. They were smoking and looked as fed up as Marianne. They must have stinking hangovers, I thought. I took a swig of water from my bottle and swatted away a fly. The rest of the tour group drifted away, along with Mohammed's voice.

Suddenly, I felt annoyed – annoyed that everyone was being so crap and negative and really annoyed that they seemed to be half-blaming me. It was hot all right, and Mohammed was the most boring man in Luxor, but I didn't want to spend the whole fortnight moping.

'It's not that bad,' I said. I looked up at the pillars. 'You've got to admit that this place is kind of impressive. I'm going to catch up with the others. We might even learn something.'

Karen threw me a sympathetic look. 'OK, I'm coming with you,' she said loyally.

Marianne shrugged. We left her with Izzy, languishing in the shade, and caught up with the back of the group.

By the time we got back to the hotel, we were all exhausted. Marianne and Izzy had trailed around after us in the end – reluctantly. I was still a bit annoyed with them, but I felt a bit bad too. This holiday was a pretty big deal for all of us, because we'd never been away together before, not on our own. I felt kind of responsible.

I thought about it as I lay on my bed in the hotel room, listening to the air-con whirring while Karen took a shower. The thing was, I told myself, Luxor was cheap. Cheap and a bit different. I'd had enough of doing the same thing, year in, year out – summer holidays with my parents and brother in France and Spain, skiing trips in the winter. And the River Nile had seemed so romantic, like something out of those old Agatha Christie movies or *Raiders of the Lost Ark*. I'd cajoled the others into it easily enough, but I never imagined they'd blame me if things weren't what they were expecting. Christ, I couldn't turn the sun off, could I?

I sighed, thinking back to how excited I'd been, seeing that weird landscape stretching out before us from the plane. And I thought of the air at sunset, dusky and warm and filled with the call to prayer from all the mosques. It was kind of beautiful and eerie all at once and sent shivers up and down my spine.

We *would* have a good time here. I'd make sure of it, one way or another, even if it meant just lying by the pool the whole frigging time. I didn't think we would, though – lie by the pool, that is. I couldn't help but think that Luxor had a lot more to offer, and not all Egyptians could be quite as bad as Elvis. Or Mohammed, for that matter.

'Let's stuff Mohammed,' I said. 'No more tours.'

The others looked at me. It was the next morning and we were lying by the pool, slowly frying. I'd finally fished out the guidebook that Mum had given me before we left.

'You mean just hang out here, by the pool?' asked Marianne. Despite all the fuss she'd been making about the heat, she's got lovely olive skin that soaks up the sun like a sponge. She turned over on to her front and peered over the top of her shades. 'Suits me.'

'Well . . .' I looked out over the Nile and watched the date palms shimmer in the heat. The pool was amazing, and couldn't have been in a better location – it actually floated on the river itself. But I didn't want to spend my entire time there. 'If you like. Or we could do some exploring ourselves.'

Marianne snorted in disbelief and flicked through her mag. 'Are you joking? It's a minefield out there.'

'Don't think she is, Mar,' said Karen, reaching for the Factor 25. 'What did you have in mind, Jen?'

I knew I could trust Karen to take an interest. And once she was up for stuff, the others would agree eventually, however much of a fuss Marianne might kick up.

'Nothing much,' I said. I waved my book at them. 'It says here that you can hire a felucca for a couple of hours to watch the sunset.'

Izzy opened one eye lazily. She'd hardly moved for about an hour, and her lanky body seemed to be lapsing into lethargy. 'What's a felucca?'

I watched as a wooden boat drifted by along the Nile. It was painted white and had benches along either side lined with colourful cushions and its single white sail soared gracefully into the sky. 'One of those,' I said, pointing.

The others looked up for a moment, then flopped back

down. 'That's one of the tours that Mohammed told us about,' observed Marianne.

'Yes,' I said, 'but the price he quoted us was crazy.'

'Sounded OK to me.' Izzy rested her head on her hands and closed her eyes.

'But we could get a much better price if we just go and get one ourselves. As long as we haggle. That's what it says here.'

Marianne gave a good-humoured groan. 'The gospel according to Jen Aston's guidebook. And guess who'll end up doing the haggling?'

She sounded like the Marianne I was used to – dry and funny and up for a challenge. I grinned at her in relief. 'You know you're good at it, Mar.'

'I'm up for it. Sounds fantastic,' said Karen. 'Another hour lying here and I'll be one of the baked bean brigade.'

We all giggled and glanced over at the other side of the pool, where the shaved heads of the lager louts were turning slowly crimson in the sun. We couldn't see a single bottle of suncream between them.


We hadn't reckoned on what would happen when we set off up the road. The night before, Mohammed had ordered a taxi to take us to the Hathor and of course we'd taken Mr Rip-Off on the way back. But now, out in the blazing sunlight, it seemed like the entire male population of Luxor had decided we were fair game. At first, the streets didn't seem particularly busy – a couple of touristy horse-drawn carriages drew up alongside us, but they weren't a problem. We ignored them and they drove on.

But then we turned on to the Corniche, the long road with Luxor temple on one side and the river with all its feluccas and cruise ships on the other. And there they were, a whole row of men lined up against the railings just like the guys had lined up around the disco. They were a mixed bunch – some in those long gowns, some in jeans, but they had one thing in common: they saw us coming. We didn't stand a chance. Four or five of them approached us instantly.

'Hey, you want felucca? You want motorboat?'

'Hey queen, lovely! Where you from? You English? England number one! How now brown cow. Such is life!'

'You very beautiful. I take you my motorboat. I give you good price. Asda price!'

'You want trip west bank? You want taxi? You want donkey? Not expensive, I show you . . .'

We walked straight ahead. They followed. We shook our heads and still they followed. It was incredible. Their eyes ate us up like we were four melting ice-creams and that's just about how we felt.

'You want fuck me?'

I spun around quickly, not even sure I'd heard right. One of the guys caught my glare and, I have to say, looked a bit ashamed. I lifted my chin and turned away. I was bewildered, shocked, and out of the corner of my eye I could see that Marianne was about to lose it.

'Get away from me!' she shrieked, as a young boy touched her elbow. 'No, I don't want your flookahs or whatever they are!'

The men laughed. Some of them jeered and I hated them. 'Cool it, Mar,' I muttered. 'Don't let them get to you.'

'Oh, like I'm supposed to take this crap!' she retorted, her cheeks scarlet for once and her green eyes snapping. 'I'm going back to the hotel.'

She meant it. I could see that, but I didn't want to give up. I looked around quickly, over the railings to the river. There was a jetty up ahead, with what looked like a ferry just pulling out. There were plenty of feluccas down there too.

'Look,' I said determinedly. 'Let's just go with one of these guys and get on a felucca. It doesn't matter which one. They can't all hassle us once we're out on the river.'

Izzy looked doubtful and almost close to tears as the vultures kept circling. Marianne was clearly speechless with rage. A young boy came up to me, his eyes far too knowing. He can't have been more than nine.

'No hassle,' he said. 'I take you to good felucca. You want go to Banana Island for sunset? Come, come. Good price.'

I glanced at the others. 'Let's just go for it,' I said. I didn't really know what to do. It was impossible to know whether any of them could be trusted. 'There are four of us. We'll be OK.'

'Come!' persisted the boy, as the other touts began to muscle him out of the way, all shouting at each other in Arabic.

Suddenly, Karen was by my side and we were walking quickly down to the jetty, following the young boy. I glanced behind me and saw that Marianne and Izzy were coming, their eyes glazed and their faces fixed. I wondered if I looked like that too. The rest of the touts fell back once they realised a deal had been struck, and before we knew it we were clambering on to a boat and being introduced to its captain.

'Ali,' he said briefly. He was tall and slender, with big eyes and a ready smile. 'Welcome to *Ali Baba* felucca. Take your time.'

We gave our names and flopped on to the cushions. With another young boy helping him, Ali pushed off from the jetty and manoeuvred the felucca out on to the river. He called out instructions in a quick, level voice and the boy we'd followed leaped around the boat like an acrobat. We peered over the sides, out to the mountain on the west bank and up and down the river. I noticed that another ferry had pulled in, and the jetty was bustling with locals getting on and off. Lots of the women carried baggage on their heads like it was perfectly normal for stuff to just balance there. I was fascinated.

After much hauling on ropes and unfurling of sails, the felucca caught the breeze and began to glide upstream, away from the hubbub of the jetty. Peace. It was obviously prime time for felucca trips, because there was a flotilla of lofty white sails further up the river, majestic and serene against the blue sky. I felt an unexpected lurch of happiness and glanced around at the others to check they were OK. Karen smiled and Izzy raised a relieved eyebrow. Marianne adjusted her shades, her expression neutral. She wouldn't look at me.

With everything under control, Ali turned his attention to us. 'You like some *shai*?' he asked. 'My cousin Mahmoud make it for you.'

We nodded and smiled, not really sure what he meant. We watched as the boy opened a hatch under the bow of the boat and reached inside it for a burner, a kettle, tea and sugar caddies and a stack of little glasses. He filled up the kettle from a bottle of water and put it to heat on the burner. No one spoke. I think we were shocked into silence after all the hassle on the Corniche, but now, slowly, we began to relax.

Steam rose from the kettle. Mahmoud spooned tealeaves into each glass and poured the water over, then added two heaped teaspoons of sugar to each. He was about to add more, but we stopped him, laughing.

He shrugged and handed out the glasses. 'You sweet enough,' he commented, his English halting. I glanced at

Ali, who was smiling. Maybe Mahmoud said that every day, I thought. Maybe it was the only English he knew.

Ali placed his own glass carefully on the bow of the boat and fished in the pocket of his long blue gown for a packet of cigarettes. I saw the brand name. Cleopatra.

'You smoke?' he asked us politely, offering them to us.

We shook our heads.

'Is bad habit,' he said gravely, fetching out a lighter. 'But everyone here smoke.'

His face calm and meditative, he flicked the lighter and lit his cigarette. He took a swig of the hot *shai*, and motioned to Mahmoud to pass him more sugar. They exchanged a few words in Arabic. I studied Ali's long blue gown that hung gracefully from his shoulders, its sleeves flaring slightly at the end. It was so simple. So elegant. I thought of the disco guys in their tight jeans and felt a flood of relief.

The felucca drifted towards the reeds and Ali scrambled around, adjusting the sail. Mahmoud took the rudder at the back and we watched as between them they managed to swing us around and out into the current again. Ali's face remained calm, and he smiled at us briefly as the felucca surged forward, its sail billowing. The smile lit up his features and I suddenly realised how good-looking he was, with his big, dark eyes and perfect teeth; I'd already noticed that tobacco and sugar took a big toll on teeth in Luxor. His black hair was close-cropped to his head, with neat sideburns that were close-cropped too. He seemed older than us but as I sized him up, I reckoned he was no more than twenty. Twenty-two, tops.

We landed on Banana Island, which didn't seem to be an island at all, though it did have plenty of banana trees. We wandered around the plantation under the protection of little Mahmoud, who stopped anyone else from approaching us. As we returned to the boat, the sun was beginning to dip, glinting on the river and silhouetting the date palms on the west bank. We sprawled out to watch the sunset as we were carried back downstream. Other feluccas were making their way back too, their sails like pale pink ghosts in the last of the fading light. The reed beds now seemed alive with the twittering of birds, and I noticed that a strange, rhythmic croaking sound was beginning to fill the air.

'What's that noise?' I asked Ali.

He smiled. 'Frogs,' he said. 'Now their time to sing.'

It reminded me of the cicadas in France and Spain, but it was somehow deeper, more exotic. Then the sun dipped down behind the palm trees, leaving us in a pink and orange afterglow, and the call to prayer rang out from all the mosques. I looked at Ali curiously. Wasn't he supposed to go and pray now? He didn't seem concerned; in fact he was concentrating on steering the felucca back towards the jetty.

Suddenly, I felt really stupid. I didn't know anything

about this country. I hadn't known what to expect and I hadn't even bothered to read the guidebook. But now I wanted to know. I wanted to find out more. I'd thought we might see a few ancient ruins, the odd mummy and some spooky tombs. But now I felt I was in another world and it was one I wanted to understand. I looked at Ali, wondering if someone like him might help me.

He caught me looking and I glanced away, feeling embarrassed. He dealt with tourists every day – he'd have better things to do than explain his life to an English girl like me. We landed at the jetty and Mahmoud helped the others out of the boat. But as I clambered forward to follow, Ali jumped on to the jetty, and reached for my hand. I took it and looked up cautiously to see his face before turning to join the others. He smiled.

This time, our eyes met.

# Chapter Two

**K**aren screamed. I was in the bedroom and I rushed to the bathroom door. 'What the –' My mouth dropped open. Karen was standing in her bra and knickers, and her thighs and upper arms were covered in little red spots.

'What is it?' she asked, staring down at herself, aghast.

I hadn't a clue. Karen looked close to tears and I nearly gave her a hug. But I didn't. I just stood there gaping, and I have to admit I wondered if it was contagious.

'Is it some tropical disease, do you think?' she managed to say, her voice barely above a whisper.

'I don't know.' I thought quickly. 'I'll go and get someone. There must be a hotel doctor or something.'

I ran down to reception, feeling scared. It hadn't crossed my mind that we might get ill here. We were on a package deal, our hotel was four-star and clean, and since we were staying full-board we weren't even eating local food. I found the hotel manager and gabbled to him incoherently.

He nodded impassively. 'Yes, yes. Many white people get this.'

'But what is it?' I couldn't believe he was so unconcerned. 'Do you have a guidebook, with a health section?'

'Yes, but . . .'

'Well, look up prickly heat. There's no point in calling a doctor. Your friend will be fine.'

I returned to our room and did as he said. There it was: prickly heat. I scanned the paragraph quickly.

'Do you itch, Karen?' I asked her.

'A bit.' Karen was still inspecting her skin as though it had turned green. She has dark hair but fairish skin, so she's always had to take it slowly in the sun. I'm the opposite – although I'm blonde, I only have to look out of a window to turn golden brown.

'It's a reaction to the heat. It'll go,' I told her.

'When?' Karen looked up at me, her face miserable.

I shrugged, wishing I could be more help. 'A few days maybe.'

Karen reached for the book and read the section. 'Great. They recommend total sun avoidance. No tan for me!' She stood up and reached for her linen trousers. 'And anyway, I'm not lying by the pool looking like this. Looks like we'll be exploring again, Jen.'

It was the morning after our felucca trip with Ali and Mahmoud. We'd come back to the hotel afterwards and spent the evening there, eating in the hotel restaurant and checking out the bar. Pretty dull, really. I'd been hoping I could persuade the others to follow the guidebook again the next day, so I was glad when Karen suggested it. Her prickly heat might look weird but it would make negotiating with Mar and Izzy a whole lot easier.

We went down for breakfast and to my surprise, they were up for it anyway. Our felucca experience had made us all a bit braver, I guess. I flicked through the guidebook and suggested the Valley of the Kings. After all, we couldn't come to Egypt without taking a peek at Tutankhamun.

'We could do that as one of Mohammed's tours,' said Izzy. 'It wouldn't be such a hassle.'

'Yeah. But we'll end up paying double,' Karen pointed out. 'We only paid Ali half what Mohammed said we'd pay. And anyway I don't think I could hack a day in the minibus. The itching would drive me crazy.'

Funny what prickly heat could do, I thought to myself. It had turned Karen from a supporter to a full-scale ambassador for independent adventures.

Marianne sniffed. 'So how would we get there?'

I checked. 'We have to cross the river on the ferry. I guess it's the one we saw yesterday. Then we get a taxi on the other side.'

We looked at each other.

'That means walking down the Corniche again.' Izzy

didn't look too happy, and cast a longing glance in the direction of the pool.

'We just ignore them,' said Karen. 'We keep walking and we ignore them.'

I stared at her in admiration. She'd really got her teeth into this. 'Too right,' I agreed. 'Let's go for it.' I gave her a grin and tried to ignore the little voice whispering in the back of my head, *Maybe we'll bump into Ali.*

It did seem easier, second time round. We walked quickly, looking straight ahead, and the touts didn't seem so persistent. I told everyone to have Egyptian pound notes at the ready and we handed them to an old man on the jetty. He counted them and nodded. We grinned at each other. We'd done it.

We walked past a couple of snack vendors and I glanced at what they were selling – little bags of pumpkin and sunflower seeds, and paper cones containing yellow Smarties-shaped beans. We stepped on board, skirted around the throbbing engine room and climbed up a little stairway on to the upper deck. The ferry was filling up slowly with local people. Most of the women stayed on the lower deck, so we were gradually surrounded by men – some in jeans but mostly dressed in those long robes. *Galabiyyas*, the guidebook called them. A lot of the older men had white scarves wrapped around their heads too, making a kind of turban.

Of course, we didn't escape their notice. We huddled on seats at the front, trying to ignore the barrage of questions from the younger guys who made a point of sitting near us.

'Where you from? Where you stay?'

'You want taxi west bank?'

'You want donkey?'

'Why you no answer?'

We looked at each other and kept our mouths shut. I could see that Marianne's temperature was rising again and I didn't really blame her. But then, I caught a glimpse of a familiar face coming up the steps and I grinned.

'Look,' I said. 'It's Ali.'

He saw us and raised his hand lazily. He wandered over.

'Where you go?' he asked. 'You go the King's Valley?'

We nodded.

'My uncle has taxi,' he said. 'I take you to him. No hassle. He give you good price. He help you buy tickets.'

'Aren't you working on the felucca?' I asked him.

'Later.' He shrugged. 'Better for sunset. This the hot time.'

It was true. It wasn't even ten o'clock yet, but the air was already like a furnace, and it was only going to get hotter. We must be crazy, heading out in the heat of the day, but somehow doing it under our own steam made it seem easier. I looked at Karen, who was scratching at her thighs through her trousers. I knew she must be uncomfortable, but I think the excitement of the unknown had got to all of us.

Ali was as good as his word. Keeping all the other taxi drivers at bay on the west bank with a few sharp words in Arabic, he led us to his uncle's car.

'This my uncle Tayib,' he told us. 'He look after you.'

We shook hands, and clambered in. I took the front seat, and wound down the window to look at Ali.

'Thank you,' I said.

'Is no problem.' He grinned. And again, our eyes met.

Tayib, like Ali, seemed quiet in comparison with most of the men we'd met. We set off up the road, passing a few little nondescript shops and a couple of cafés where men sat outside drinking *shai* and smoking. I noticed an Internet café, which somehow seemed odd. Then, in no time at all, we were out in the fields, which stretched out in a flat expanse towards the golden-pink mountains.

Tayib said little, only pointing to two bizarre ancient statues that rose out of the plain. There was a tour bus parked in front of them and I saw people clicking away with their cameras, surrounded by local guys waving postcards and sheets of papyrus. I felt a thrill of excitement that we weren't in a tour group any more, and flicked through the book to find out what the statues were. I told the others, 'Colossi of Memnon. They're all that's left of a huge ancient temple.' I was getting into this.

Tayib helped us buy our tickets at a little shack in the middle of nowhere, then we piled into the car again. We were right under the mountain now, which was dotted with mud-brick houses, some painted yellow or blue. I saw a kid in the cutest little *galabiyya* chasing a couple of skinny goats, and I wondered what it was like to grow up here. It was strange how desolate the landscape had become now that we'd left the fields – this place seemed surreal, all parched yellow-white rocks and dust, and I remembered once more that view from the plane. This was the desert: not a plant in sight.

We caught sight of an amazing temple beneath the cliffs.

'Temple Hatshepsut,' Tayib informed us. He gave a shy little grin. 'Hot Chicken Soup,' he added, as though it was a cracking joke, and we laughed politely.

We drove past a cluster of alabaster factories – Isis for Alabaster, Anubis Alabaster – and then we were driving up, up through a deserted desert valley between golden craggy outcrops, away from all the houses and temples. The road wound on until we saw a row of shining tour buses, and we realised we'd arrived at the Valley of the Kings.

We'd decided to visit just three of the tombs. It was pretty obvious we'd be almost dead from the heat after that. Tutankhamun was our number one choice, of course, then we'd had a brief squabble over the others. In the end, Seti I won because his tomb was supposed to be best, and Tuthmosis III because we'd have to scramble up through the limestone cliffs to get there, which sounded like a bit of a challenge.

We began our exploration. Even here, we were getting hassle, this time from all the old guides who wanted money for stating the totally obvious. '*Baksheesh, baksheesh*,' they all muttered, and it didn't take a genius to work out that it was some kind of tip they were after. I'd begun to relax a bit, so I noticed that a lot of them had a wicked twinkle in their eye. I soon found that if you joked with them, they roared with laughter.

With Tutankhamun and Seti behind us, we made for the cleft in the rocks and the hidden tomb of Tuthmosis. I think it was there, climbing up through that narrow crevice like Indiana Jones, that I fell in love. Not with any of the men, who were mostly beyond the pale as far as I was concerned – but with the place itself. Golden limestone towering above us, secret passageways, and then these amazing painted tombs made thousands of years before. Inside, we stared up at a ceiling painted with stars, then looked at each other in awe. Without the tour group and Mohammed droning on, it felt like a real adventure. We grinned, wiped away the streams of sweat, and glugged from our water bottles. It felt like the four of us were back on track: at last, we were having fun.

Back down at the riverside, Tayib struck a hard bargain. I was kind of surprised. Ali had been a gentle negotiator but his uncle was tough. As Marianne dug her heels in and haggled, I found myself feeling torn. I was proud of Mar, and glad we finally seemed to be getting the hang of it all. But as Tayib told us we were taking food from his children I felt a pang. I looked around uneasily. I wasn't sure why, but I didn't want Ali to witness this. I didn't want him to think we were mean.

So, of course, I spotted him before the others did.

'Hi, *ya* Jen,' he greeted me, those dark eyes searching for mine.

I wasn't sure what the *ya* meant, but I liked the sound of it. I guess I blushed. He smiled and listened to the negotiations.

'This OK. This good price,' he intervened, agreeing to Mar's suggestion. I was surprised, and watched as he spoke rapidly in Arabic to Tayib.

His uncle glared at him. There was an awkward silence.

'Well . . .' said Mar. 'That's great.'

'Let's pay five extra,' I muttered to the others. '*Baksheesh.*'

'*Five?*' exclaimed Marianne. 'I've just managed to get him down to a sensible price!'

'I don't think you did, Mar,' I said, throwing a quick glance at Ali. It was obvious that Tayib would have haggled for longer if it hadn't been for him.

Tayib spat on the ground, and turned away. We handed our money to Ali, who touched his uncle on the shoulder and persuaded him to accept. With a shrug, Tayib stuffed the notes into the pocket of his *galabiyya*. He turned to look at us again, for a moment. His expression was strange.

I felt bewildered. I didn't want to upset this man but I didn't understand the rules. Ali seemed sure we'd paid enough. I smiled nervously. 'Thank you,' I said. 'We'll use your taxi again.'

The others had walked away.

'Come on, Jen. Looks like the ferry's about to go,' called Karen.

I hesitated, then smiled at Ali and turned to follow the others. I was fishing for an Egyptian pound note to pay for the ferry when someone touched my elbow and I looked up. Ali had followed me.

'You like to come see me later?' he asked. 'Here, on west bank. Your friends also. We make . . .' He waggled his finger up and down, then showed a seam on his *galabiyya* by way of illustration. 'We fix for felucca.'

'You mend the sail?' I guessed.

He nodded, grinning.

'Jen! Come on! It's going!' cried Izzy from the ferry landing.

I shoved the pound note in the ferryman's hand. 'Where? What time?' I called to Ali.

'Here. Eight o'clock,' he replied, and waved as I made a run for the ferry.

'Are you totally crazy?' Marianne's voice was

incredulous. 'You are not seriously thinking of going, are you?'

I looked at Karen, then back at Marianne. 'He invited us, Mar.'

'Oh, and that makes it OK, does it? You'll just trot off with any Tom, Dick or Mohammed who *invites* you somewhere?'

I looked down and played with my plate of chips. It did my head in, being on the receiving end of Mar's sarcasm. I wasn't used to it.

We were back at the hotel having a late lunch. I'd waited until we'd got back to tell the others about Ali's invite, thinking it might go down better in a cool, safe atmosphere. The truth was, I was nervous myself. Ali seemed lovely and I was sure I could trust him, but the idea of heading over the river at night was pretty scary all the same.

I took a deep breath. 'He said to meet him on the ferry landing. We can head straight back if it's dodgy.' I sounded a lot more confident than I felt.

'You're losing it, Jen. We've had one nice felucca trip and a taxi ride to the tombs. That's it. You know what all the men have been like so far, and just because Ali twisted his uncle's arm for us doesn't make him different. You don't know what he's after. He could have a whole load of mates ready to relieve you of your valuables or . . . or . . .' Mar trailed off significantly.

'We won't take our frigging valuables.' It was a dim

thing to say, but Mar was getting my back up. It really rattled me that she wasn't on my side. What was worse, her words made a lot of sense, and I didn't want to admit it.

'*You* won't take them, you mean.' Mar glared at me. 'I'm not going. I can't believe you're really this stupid. Christ.'

Silence fell.

I looked at Izzy, though I knew it was hopeless. She'd always stick by Mar. I wondered if Mar was right. Maybe it *was* stupid to trust Ali. But Mum always told me to trust my instincts, and my instincts told me he was OK.

'I'll come with you.' Karen's voice broke through my thoughts and I looked at her in disbelief. Her face was surprisingly calm. 'I know you, Jen. If you don't go, you'll spend the rest of the summer wondering what might have happened if you did. But you can't go on your own. The two of us will go and we'll take our mobiles. If anything happens, the others can raise the alarm here.'

She made it sound like we were heading out on some trans-Saharan expedition instead of across the River Nile on the ferry. And funnily enough, it made me want to go all the more. It was a lot more exciting than hanging around in the hotel bar. I reached across and gave her a hug.

'You're a star, Karen,' I told her. I looked at the others. In spite of my excitement, it didn't feel right going off without them. We'd always stuck together until now. 'We'll give you a blow by blow account when we get back,' I said awkwardly.

Izzy smiled. 'Hope it's fun,' she said quietly.

I looked at Mar. She raised an eyebrow, and shrugged.

'You're a nutter, Jen,' she said. But to my relief, she gave me a little smile too.

When the time came, it was all so much easier than we'd expected. The daytime touts had disappeared, leaving only the drivers of the horse-drawn carriages to pester us along the Corniche. We hurried down to the jetty and sat on the lower deck of the ferry, amongst some women. They looked at us with open curiosity and I wondered what they made of us, two Western girls heading over the river at night. As far as I could tell, there weren't many places for tourists to stay on the west bank. The main town with all the big hotels was on the east.

The ferry chugged over the quiet waters, and the twinkling lights of the west bank drew closer. I peered out at the dark figures near the jetty, wondering which of them was Ali. It was hard to tell from a distance, because they all wore *galabiyyas*. As the ferry pulled in, I feared for an awful moment that he wouldn't be there at all.

But he was. He was standing on his own, his *galabiyya* blowing against his lean body, the tip of his Cleopatra glowing in the dark. I felt a stupid grin spread over my face and I waved. He spotted us and waved back, and I could see he was grinning too.

Karen squeezed my arm. 'So far, so good,' she muttered,

as we stepped on to the jetty. 'No sign of the hit squad yet.'

Ali came towards us, looking oddly shy. 'Your friends?' he asked. 'They no come?'

We shook our heads. 'They are tired,' I said.

'Yes, Egypt make tired. Too much hassle. But I am glad you come. Come, my friends this way.'

He indicated along the shore, away from the jetty, where the banks of the Nile stretched away to the south and down towards the reed beds. There were motorboats moored there and the odd felucca. Men called out to us as we walked and were rebuked by Ali. I grinned at Karen. Now that I was here, I felt safe.

Ali led us to a group of three or four men, sitting cross-legged with a felucca sail stretched between them. Two of them were sewing, using thick four-inch long needles. I stared. It was such an odd scene. I don't know what I'd imagined when Ali had said they were mending the sail, but somehow it hadn't been this. They were all smoking, talking, laughing – a little domesticated party on the riverbank.

An older man stood up to greet us.

'Welcome,' he said, smiling and shaking our hands. 'Welcome in Egypt.'

'This my father, Ibrahim,' said Ali. '*Ali Baba* his felucca.'

His father! I resisted the urge to raise an eyebrow at Karen and nodded and smiled instead.

'You drink *shai*?' asked Ibrahim.

'Er – no, it's OK . . .' I began.

Ali's father would hear none of it. 'Yes, yes, you drink *shai* with us. *Ya* Mahmoud!'

The young boy appeared from further up the bank, where he was chatting to friends of his own. Ali's father shouted instructions to him and he scampered off, returning a few minutes later with two little glasses of sweet strong tea. We thanked him.

'Is no problem,' Mahmoud said, with a coy smile, and I figured he knew more English than he let on.

The fine shingle of the shore was dry, so Karen and I sat down with our glasses of *shai*. From here we could see Luxor temple, its golden pillars lit up by floodlights, and the lights from the river cruisers twinkling on the water. Another friend of Ali's appeared with a portable ghetto blaster. He checked us over with brief curiosity, then turned on a tape of Arabic pop music. We hugged our knees, and listened as the wailing drifted out. The batteries were going, but it still sounded amazing.

'You OK, *ya* Jen?' Ali sat down next to me and the friend with the ghetto blaster started talking to Karen.

'Great,' I said. 'Thanks for asking us, Ali.'

'I was afraid,' he said gravely. 'I think you not come.'

I laughed, a bit nervously. 'Well – we're here,' I said.

'How long you stay?'

'Just two weeks.'

Ali shook his head. 'Never enough,' he said.

I wasn't sure what he meant – did he mean there was never enough time, with tourists? I felt a clutch of fear. Maybe he was always asking girls to come and join him on the west bank. In fact, it was pretty likely. I mentally kicked myself for being so stupid.

But then he asked me about my life in England and what I would do when I went back. He asked about my family. I began to talk, and as he listened, my fears dissolved. He was good to talk to. Maybe he *did* talk to lots of tourists, but suddenly I didn't care. It was me he was with right now.

'How about you?' I asked him. 'Do you study too?'

Ali shook his head. 'My family need me. I work the felucca.'

'But you said it was your father's boat.'

'Yes, but he is many times sick. I do the work now. And no brothers . . . this why I am not in the army.'

I didn't know what he was talking about. 'The army?'

'Every Egyptian man must go in the army. For three years, or one if you finish the school. You not know this?'

It seemed incredible. 'But you haven't gone,' I said. I frowned. 'Because you have no brothers, did you say?'

Ali nodded. 'Many sisters,' he said, smiling. 'Egypt government very strong,' he said. 'We have big army. But in this way, I have luck. I stay here.'

'I'm glad.' I glanced at him quickly.

'Me also.'

We lapsed into silence. I looked round at Karen and saw that she wasn't chatting any more, but was gazing out over the river. I caught her eye and could tell that she was doing fine. Happy, in fact.

'You come with me to a wedding, tomorrow night?' Ali asked me.

'A *wedding*?' I stared at him. 'I haven't been invited.'

'Just small. Village wedding. Music. Anyone go. I take you and your friends, if you like. You come and eat with my family, then we go.'

I stared at him. 'Are you sure? In England, you have to know the people getting married.'

Ali grinned and shook his head. 'Not here,' he said. 'This not England, *ya* Jen.'

I hesitated, wondering what the others would make of it. Mar would probably have a fit. 'Well . . . thank you. I'll think about it,' I said. I smiled, and decided to change the subject. 'What does *ya* mean?' I asked.

Ali looked surprised. '*Ya?*'

'Yes. Like you just said to me, *ya* Jen.'

Ali looked baffled, like he hadn't even noticed he'd said it. He thought for a moment, then shrugged. 'Always like this way. I call a person, I say *ya*. *Ya* Mahmoud, *ya* Nasser . . . *ya* Jen. This what we say.'

I nodded. 'I like it,' I said.

Ali leaned a little closer. My heart beat slightly faster,

and our eyes locked for a second. He hesitated, and I thought he was about to say more. But then he drew back, looking slightly bashful, and scrambled to his feet. 'I get you more *shai*,' he said, and disappeared into the darkness.

And so the evening passed. None of the others came on to us. They offered us cigarettes and talked amongst themselves. We basked in the warm night air until the work on the sail was completed and we thought we had better get back. Ali said that if we wanted to go to the wedding, we should meet him on the jetty at eight o'clock the following evening.

'You know what,' said Karen, as we sat on the ferry and watched the figure of Ali growing smaller.

'What?'

She draped her arm around my shoulder. 'Well . . . I was watching you this evening. You and Ali.'

I grinned. 'Yeah. Listening too, I bet.'

'Of course.'

We giggled. Even if she hadn't been listening, she knew I'd tell her every last detail. 'So what do you reckon then?' I asked, dying to know what she thought.

Karen paused, keeping me waiting. 'Well . . .' she said slowly, and her face grew serious. 'I get the feeling . . .'

'*What?*' The suspense was killing me.

Karen grinned and punched my arm. 'Top marks, Aston. I reckon he's OK.'

# Chapter Three

You know how you can tell when mates have been talking about you? You walk into the room and they give you this look, as though they suddenly know you better than you know yourself. Well, that's the feeling I got when we walked into the hotel bar to find Mar and Izzy waiting for us.

I was pretty full of it. I tried not to be triumphant but I couldn't help crowing, at bit. Mar and Izzy still had this knowing, conspiratorial air about them but I didn't care, I was flying too high. Then Karen gave me a nudge and I piped down. We went to bed.

The next morning, Mar and Izzy behaved like we hadn't been out on a nocturnal adventure across the river at all. They just wouldn't talk about it. It was weird. After breakfast, they announced that they were going to get some sunbathing in by the pool.

'Great,' said Karen, when she and Izzy had gone. 'So what am I supposed to do? Show off my spots to the lager louts?'

'Maybe we could just go and lounge around with our mags for a bit,' I suggested. I chewed my lip. This difference of opinion thing was getting out of hand. 'It's not like Mar to be this huffy. I don't want to fall out.'

Karen looked thoughtful. 'To be honest, Jen, I think she's jealous.'

'*Jealous*?'

'Well . . . you remember what she said on the way from the airport. I think she was really hoping for a bit of action here.'

My mouth dropped open. 'But not *Egyptian* . . . action.' I wasn't sure I liked referring to Ali as *action* – even if that's what he was, and I didn't really know, yet.

Karen shrugged. 'Same difference. Doesn't matter who. She's the one sitting painting her nails while you have all the fun.'

'But . . .' I stuttered. 'This is *Mar* we're talking about.'

'I've just got this theory,' said Karen. 'At home, she's got this whole thing about looking down at guys and making fun of them. She's never going to break out of it there, or at least not till she goes to uni. But I reckon she's fed up of being an ice queen and I bet she was hoping to get a bit of practice here. And now you've beaten her to it, as usual.' She smiled wryly. 'Think about it, Jen.'

I did think about it, lying beside the pool. I couldn't believe that Mar saw me as a rival. It just wasn't supposed to be an issue. We'd got our roles sorted out years ago in our little group. Karen had been going out with Stef since she was sixteen and Izzy was always trying to pretend she wasn't in love with Reuben, this guy in our year. But Mar . . . Mar kept guys at arm's length. It was what she was famous for. And I didn't. It was simple. I'd always had boyfriends, from when I was about thirteen. Two of them had lasted a year and there had been a whole string of shorter flings. To be honest, by the time I'd left school I was feeling bored with the lot of them.

But what Karen said made sense. Of course Mar couldn't carry on the way she was forever. She had to break out of it somehow and maybe I wasn't helping seeing Ali. But was that really *my* fault?

I was looking across at Mar and Izzy, puzzling it out and wondering if I should try to talk it over, when a shadow fell across my face and I looked up. There was a tall girl standing there with long light brown hair, wearing a pale blue bikini.

'You mind if I join you?' She had an accent that I couldn't place, but her English was perfect.

I shook my head and moved my towel and suncream off the next sun lounger. She flopped down on to it.

'I'm Lisa,' she said.

We didn't chat right away. Lisa just stretched out and basked in the sun. But when we did start talking, I was intrigued. She was German and had spent a lot of time in Luxor.

'It's crazy – to be here now,' she said. 'Too hot. Most of the Westerners go home for the summer.'

'You mean the people who live here?'

'The *women* who live here.' Lisa gave me a sly grin.

I didn't know what she was getting at. 'Don't Western men live here too?'

Lisa reached for her suncream and began smearing it on to her perfect brown legs. 'I was joking,' she said. 'Sure, there are men. But most of them are gay.'

I still felt a bit confused, so I said nothing.

'You know, Luxor is not just about temples and tombs,' Lisa carried on. She made a little scratching motion with her finger. 'You don't have to dig very far to find the dirt. It's a . . .' She searched for the right words. 'It's a pit of snakes.'

I thought of the sleazy nightclub and the men on the Corniche. 'I know that,' I said.

Lisa snapped the lid of her suncream shut. She looked at me. 'Do you?' she asked softly. 'The men here . . .' She shrugged. 'You must be careful.'

There was something about the way she said it that made me feel cold in the pit of my stomach. She couldn't possibly know about Ali but it felt spooky, having a total stranger speak to me like that. To my relief, I saw Karen beckoning from the doorway – she'd stayed inside to read with the air-con, as she said it stopped the prickly heat from itching so much. I jumped up from my lounger.

'I've just got to speak to my friend,' I said. 'Good to meet you, Lisa.'

Lisa gave a lazy smile, nodded and lay back on the lounger. I grabbed my towel and suncream and headed for the door.

'What is it?' I asked Karen as we headed back to our room.

'Just getting a bit bored,' she replied. 'And I've been wondering if we should get something to wear for later on.'

'Wear? What do you mean?'

'Well, it'll be a traditional Muslim wedding, right? The bride will probably be covered from head to toe in one of those *burqa* things and we've no idea what the guests should wear. I just thought we should get ourselves some headscarves from the market or *souq* or whatever it's called. Just in case.'

'Blimey, Karen, I hadn't even thought about it.' I sat down on the bed and reached for the guidebook, then flung it to one side. It wasn't going to be much help on village wedding etiquette. 'I guess you're right. And we haven't been around the *souq* yet anyway. Could be fun.'

I'd told Karen about the wedding invite on the way back the night before. She'd thought it was fantastic and said right away that we should go. But somehow, we hadn't managed to tell Mar and Izzy. Now, the same thought must have crossed our minds at the same time because we gave each other this funny look.

'What about the others?' I said.

'Yeah,' said Karen. 'Well, let's ask them if they want to come to the *souq* with us.'

Somehow I knew they wouldn't, and I was right. Neither Mar nor Izzy wanted anything to do with my 'escapade', as Mar called it. They said they were going to stay by the pool and look around Luxor temple later. There was definitely tension building and I didn't like it, but I didn't know what to do about it either. We'd never been in a situation like this before. It was as though being here had upset the balance between us. I knew I should probably try to talk it over but I didn't really feel like trying to justify myself. I thought Ali was lovely and Karen was backing me all the way. Whatever happened, he was showing us stuff we'd never have seen otherwise. Besides, I just didn't understand how Mar and Izzy could hang out by the pool so much. Like Karen, I was getting bored.

We headed off to the *souq* after lunch. It consisted of one narrow street and few side streets in central Luxor, packed with stalls selling every imaginable souvenir – statues of gods, pyramids, *galabiyyas*, mounds of colourful spices, you name it. I reckon we picked the right time of day – it was still ridiculously hot and most of the stalls weren't even attended. We caught glimpses of men sitting in the back of shops, looking lethargic, smoking fags or those big hubble-bubble pipes. *Sheeshas*, they called them.

A few of them tried the usual lines, but we could tell their hearts weren't in it, so it didn't take long to find someone who'd sell us a couple of scarves. Without Mar, we probably paid too much, but we were proud of our haggling all the same.

I got more jittery as the evening approached. Maybe it was the weird feeling that Lisa had given me, the atmosphere around Mar and Izzy or the thought of seeing Ali again. We spent what seemed like hours in our room, trying different ways of wearing the scarves. I was just tying mine under my hair at the back when Izzy put her head around the door.

'Are you coming down to dinner?' she asked.

'Er . . . no,' I replied. 'Ali asked us to eat with him.'

Izzy's face fell.

'You could still come, if you wanted,' I told her. I hesitated, then added, 'You don't have to listen to Mar the whole time.'

It was the wrong thing to say. Izzy glared at me. 'Mar's right,' she said. 'It's really crazy to get involved here. Neither of us would have come if we'd known it was going to be like this.'

'Like *what*?' I snapped back. 'What are you talking about? All we've done is get out there and be friendly to –'

'Hey, hey,' Karen cut across me. 'It's no big deal, Izzy. We're doing one thing, you and Mar are doing another. We don't have to fall out over it, do we?'

Myself and Izzy looked at each other for a long, hard moment.

'I just hope you know what you're doing, Jen,' said Izzy eventually. And then she left, closing the door behind her.

It was almost time for us to go and I didn't want to think about Mar and Izzy. I just blocked it out. We concentrated on sorting out what to wear, picking our baggiest long-sleeved cotton shirts and tying the headscarves under our chins, like all the women seemed to do here. It was fun, but all the same I had a kind of bitter-sweet feeling in my stomach as we set out for the ferry.

This time, seeing Ali waiting for us on the jetty, I felt my insides lurch. I wasn't ready for it. It was like when a lift drops too suddenly and everything churns over – only nicer. Much, much nicer. Then, when we got closer, there was that big exchange of grins that just won't fade even when you want it to. I gripped Karen's arm.

'We go this way.' Ali smiled, then led us quickly up some steps to what seemed like a big bus terminal, only it was full of pick-ups instead, each with benches down either side in the back. Ali picked one out and told us to climb in. It was already half-full with men and women, but they shuffled up willingly as we peered in and clambered up beside them. Comments flew around in Arabic and I knew they were talking about us. But they were friendly and let us sit in peace. I remember thinking, *This is* real *Egypt*.

Ali joined us and the pick-up clattered off. I felt a thrill of excitement. I'd never done anything like this before. We were heading right off the tourist trail and I never thought it would feel so brilliant, which it would have been even if Ali's thigh hadn't been pressing lightly against my own. Which it was.

When someone knocked the glass window that separated us from the cab, the pick-up ground to a halt. People clambered in and out. Curious looks were thrown our way and questions were answered by Ali. Then it was our turn, and we tumbled out on to a narrow road. I suddenly realised that Ali was paying the driver, and I rummaged for money.

'No, no,' he said, waving it away. 'I pay for you. Forget it.'

It certainly made a change, but it made me feel guilty too. Karen and I followed Ali down a little lane to a cluster of mud-brick houses. We turned in through a doorway and into a courtyard, then entered a simple room.

It was a bit of a shock. I hadn't realised how basic it would be. There was hardly any furniture – just a couple of benches lined with cushions, and a table with a TV on it in one corner. The floor was just compacted earth; the mud-brick walls were painted egg-shell blue and were adorned with a few pictures – a poster of a football team, a framed piece of Arabic calligraphy (I guessed it was from the Koran), and another framed photo of someone I didn't recognise.

'Sit, sit,' Ali instructed us, then disappeared, calling to someone further into the house.

We did as he said, looking around the room a bit awkwardly.

'I wonder if this is where we'll eat,' I muttered. 'There's no table though.'

Karen giggled nervously. 'Maybe the women have to size us up first.'

But there was no sign of the women, although we could hear their voices, chattering loudly somewhere. Suddenly, Ali's father Ibrahim appeared, all smiles, and shook our hands.

'Welcome, welcome,' he said. 'You eat with us?'

Karen and I looked at each other. 'I think so,' I said.

'Good, good,' said Ibrahim. 'The food come.'

Ali came in with a girl following him. She carried a tray of food, which she placed in the middle of the floor. She looked shyly at us, smiling widely, then skipped out of the room again quickly. Ali squatted down on the floor, cross-legged, and gestured to us. 'Come, sit. I hope you hungry.'

Ibrahim sat down next to him and we did as we were told. I wondered if we should take our scarves off while we ate, but then decided against it. Ali handed me a round loaf. 'You like bread? My grandmother make it,' he said.

'Thank you,' I replied, and hesitated before tearing off a chunk and passing it on to Karen. I stared at the food and wondered what effect it would have on our stomachs. The chicken pieces looked edible enough, and the pasta, but I wasn't so sure about the rest. Ibrahim was already dunking his bread in some green slimy stuff that looked disgusting.

'You try this,' he suggested.

'What is it?' I asked doubtfully.

'*Molokhiya*,' he replied, which wasn't much help.

I looked anxiously at Ali, who grinned. 'This *fuul*,' he said, pointing to a dish of what looked like greyish baked beans floating in oil. He picked it up and mashed the beans with a fork. Apart from a couple of spoons stuck into the dish of pasta, there wasn't any other cutlery. It was dunk and dip all the way. I watched for a moment, then dunked my bread in the beans, which turned out to be surprisingly tasty.

My mind was racing. Where were the women? Was this a special meal served on our behalf? Ali and Ibrahim seemed to watch our every mouthful. We did our best to eat heartily but it was difficult. I was aware of whispering outside the door, and caught a glimpse of two little girls, peeking in at us.

'Doesn't your mother eat with you?' I asked Ali eventually.

'No, no,' he said, laughing. 'She eat with the children. You my guests.'

I didn't really see what difference that should make. I felt uncomfortable.

'I think he means we're honorary men,' murmured Karen.

Ibrahim insisted we eat more of the chicken, while giving us his views on the Egyptian President, Mubarak, who it turned out was the guy in the picture on the wall. We smiled and nodded, picking nervously at the chicken. I was relieved when one of the girls finally took the tray away. Ibrahim stood up and stretched, then sat down on one of the benches and offered us cigarettes. We shook our heads. The door opened and a woman came in carrying a tray of glasses of *shai*.

'This my mother,' said Ali.

We stood up hurriedly and I gazed curiously at this shy, slightly plump woman, who looked years younger than my own mum. She placed the tray on the table next to the TV and shook our hands.

Ali grinned. 'She no speak English,' he said.

I wished she did – or that I spoke Arabic. We couldn't even say hello properly.

'How do I say thank you?' I asked Ali.

'*Shokran*,' he told me.

I turned to the woman. '*Sh . . . shokran*,' I repeated, and Karen did the same. It had an instant effect. For a split second, Ali's mum gave us a brilliant smile.

'*Afwan*,' she replied.

'You're welcome,' Ali translated.

Then she bobbed her head at us and slipped out of the room. We drank our *shai*, and I noticed that Ali didn't smoke in front of his father. I wondered why not. I felt swamped, totally overwhelmed by so much difference. I threw quick glances at Karen for reassurance, and longer ones at Ali. Our eyes met often over that scalding hot *shai*. And each time they did, in spite of my confusion, my heart seemed to lurch a bit further.

A car horn sounded outside and Ali jumped to his feet.

'This our taxi,' he told us. 'My friend Sharif. Come, we go to the party.'

We said our goodbyes to Ibrahim, with many *shokrans* thrown in.

'You come again, *insh'allah*,' he said to us. Then he looked at me. 'Ali is good man,' he said, in a gentle voice. 'Very good man.'

I was glad that he said it – and said it to me. But I didn't know what to say in reply. So I just followed Ali and Karen outside, where one of those pick-up service taxis was waiting. This time, there were no locals inside. Sharif, it seemed, was off-duty.

'You go in the front,' said Ali, so we piled in and said hello to Sharif, a weedy guy with a moustache and a cheeky smile. 'His English not so good. He no work with tourists.'

'England number one,' Sharif commented. He gave us a thumbs-up. 'Lovely jubbly.'

Ali slammed the door shut after us and went round to the back, where his face appeared through the glass behind us.

'*Yalla*. We go,' said Sharif, and pulled away with a squeal of tyres.

So we were off, heading into the night down little rural lanes, away from Luxor civilisation as we knew it. Karen and I nudged each other, grinning in sheer excitement.

'I wonder if our mobiles work out here?' whispered Karen.

I sniggered. 'Do you care?'

She laughed. 'Not much.'

I looked back at Ali, and resisted the urge to blow him a kiss.

We bounced over potholes into a village festooned with coloured lights. Sharif parked near the square and we joined the throng. It seemed like the entire population of the village was sitting around on benches or down on the matting that had been laid out. Kids were running around everywhere. In one corner, in a kind of bower, sat the bride and groom. We stared. This wasn't what we'd been expecting. A *burqa*? No way! The bride was dressed in a short-sleeved cream and silver meringue and her face was plastered with pale make-up. Her head was uncovered and her long black hair cascaded over her shoulders. To top off the effect, the groom was wearing a suit and tie. It made me feel pretty daft, wearing that hot, itchy headscarf, I can tell you.

But as we looked around, we realised that no one else had abandoned their usual dress. The women were wearing headscarves and were all sitting together, laughing, chatting and telling off their kids. The men were in their everyday *galabiyyas* and, most striking of all, there weren't any other Westerners in sight.

'Come, come,' Ali said to us. 'My friends this way. The music start very soon.'

He picked his way through the crowd, greeting and hugging some people and waving to others. People smiled at me and Karen as though we were long-lost relatives and a few of the women tried to make us sit with them. We laughed and shook our heads, keeping close on Ali's heels. A space miraculously appeared on a bench in front of us as Ali's friends moved to make room. We sat down and looked around.

The bride and groom were now on the far side of the square from us. Up in front, I realised there was a makeshift stage, where some musicians were assembling their gear and testing their mikes. Ali sat down next to me and I leaned my shoulder against his.

'Is this a famous band?' I asked him.

He laughed. 'Good. Not famous. They play music of Upper Egypt.'

I vaguely remembered from the guidebook that Upper

Egypt was in fact the south. Here, in other words. He told us that the drums were *tablas* and that the strange stringed instrument was an *oud*. The singer grasped a microphone and they began to play. The music was pretty different to the Arabic pop music we'd heard before. To my ears, it was all a bit of a tuneless wail, but the atmosphere was fantastic and I couldn't believe what a great time we were having.

Ali leaned towards me, his eyes twinkling.

'You very beautiful in this scarf,' he said. But his mouth was twitching and I knew he was kidding me.

'You think so?' I said. 'What about Karen?'

'Two beautiful Egyptian girls,' he said, glancing at her, then at his friends who were talking to her. 'We call you Fatima and Amira.' Now he really was laughing and I felt confused.

'We didn't know . . .' I began. Then our eyes met and I started laughing too. 'We wanted to do the right thing.'

'I know,' he said, more seriously. 'I joke with you, but really, this make me very happy. Thank you, *ya* Jen.' And carefully, so that no one could see, he placed his arm around me and gently squeezed.

Things began to hot up, and some of the guys starting to dance in front of the band.

'They're *belly dancing*,' muttered Karen in my ear, incredulous.

They were as well – all these guys in their *galabiyyas*.

And they were naturals at it too, shaking and rotating their hips, fooling around and hugging each other. They grinned at us and beckoned. But I had one eye on the group of women sitting apart, and thought I'd better stay where I was. Not that I can belly dance, anyway.

'You happy?' Ali asked me, noticing my reluctance.

I nodded, and laughed. 'You bet.'

It was so true, and suddenly I wished the others were with us. They're two of my best mates and it seemed crazy that we'd fallen out over this. Here we were, having a brilliant time while they were stuck in the hotel. *That's it*, I thought. I decided to persuade them to join in with my 'escapade' if it was the last thing I did.

And then Karen gave me a nudge. 'Wasn't that the girl lying next to you by the pool today?'

I looked across the square. Lisa was with three local guys, and she was looking our way. 'Yeah,' I said. 'Lisa.' I wasn't sure I wanted to know what she thought of us being here. But *she* was with Egyptian guys, wasn't she? *You must be careful*, she'd said. But she didn't look like she was being so careful herself.

She'd spotted us and was making her way over. I wondered if she knew Ali, but if she did, she didn't let on. She just told us that she'd heard about the band playing from her west bank friends and had decided to come over. It was obviously true that weddings were open to everyone.

Lisa got chatting to Karen while I talked to Ali. The German girl seemed to know so much about life here, and I kept one ear tuned in to their conversation. It turned out that she wasn't staying at the Horizon; she just paid to use its pool. In fact, she wasn't staying in a hotel at all – she was renting a flat, right in the centre of town. *Wow,* I thought. *She's* one of those women that she talked about. And I was intrigued to know her story, because there sure as dammit had to be one.

The night wore on. I didn't want to leave, but it was getting pretty late and I knew we should be getting back. I spoke to Ali and he beckoned to Sharif.

'Can I get a lift with you guys?' Lisa asked us.

'Sure,' I said.

We walked to the pick-up – myself and Ali, Sharif, Karen and Lisa. When we got there, we realised there wasn't room for us three girls in the front.

'I'll get in the back, with Ali,' I said quickly.

I hadn't realised how badly I wanted to be alone with him until then. But he must have felt the same way, because it was only seconds after climbing in and out of sight that we wrapped our arms around each other. This time, it wasn't just our eyes that got to meet.

# Chapter Four

I was so happy I wanted to burst, and I wanted the others to burst with me. I hardly slept – I just lay in bed, staring at the ceiling, reliving every moment in the back of that pick-up: how we'd been thrown around going over potholes and round bends and how we'd barely noticed, or hadn't cared anyway. I wanted to tell the whole world.

But the next morning, eating Corn Flakes in the Horizon restaurant, the normality of it was like a slap with a wet fish. Mar and Izzy were in a better mood. They'd booked to go and see the Sound and Light show that night at Karnak. Until then, they were going to spend the day quietly by the pool. They had hangovers, but they'd had fun last night. There had been a covers band playing in the hotel bar and they'd sunk God knows how many Bacardi Breezers between them.

So it looked like they'd decided to get on with their holiday on their own, without us. It was weird, though –

like they were in a world I no longer belonged to. And I tell you what, it hurt. Everything seemed to have changed, and before I knew it, I'd opened my mouth and spilled everything out. Yeah. Everything.

I just wanted them to be glad for me and talk it over, like we would if we were at home. I couldn't understand why they wouldn't. It was really obvious that Ali was fantastic, and that he was giving both me and Karen a once-in-a-lifetime experience. But all the same, they didn't want to know.

Mar took a deep breath. 'Jen,' she said. 'We've only got nine days left here and you're talking about this guy like he's your fiancé.'

'Well . . .' I hesitated. 'I think Ali's pretty special, as a matter of fact.'

'Don't be stupid. You only met him three days ago.'

I stared at Marianne. I felt a choking feeling in my throat and I wanted to lash out at her. But she had more to say. A lot more.

'All those guys,' she said, 'all of them – the ones who work on feluccas and donkeys and motorboats and taxis – they meet a different bunch of tourists every week. Can't you see that?'

*Ali's different*, I wanted to say. But I could see how that would sound so I waited, thinking, while Mar kept on bulldozing.

'They're all after something,' she carried on, like some

goddamn terrier that just won't let go. 'They're after money or cheap sex or . . . or passports to get them out of here. They haven't got any respect for Western women and you can't blame them. And you're just falling for it. I bet Ali saw you coming a mile off – a nice, naïve blonde . . .'

'Just shut it, Mar.' I glared at her.

She stopped. The fact was she'd gone too far, and she knew it. I would have accepted all the stuff about the money and the passports and the sex. It was all true – you didn't have to be a brain surgeon to work it out. Anyway, Lisa had said pretty much the same.

'So what makes you such an expert all of a sudden, Mar?' I asked her, keeping my voice nice and casual. 'You're now not only an expert on men but on *Egyptian* men. Since when, exactly?' Sure, it was cruel, but I had to defend myself somehow. I didn't dare look at Karen or Izzy.

Mar's cheeks flushed scarlet. 'Don't be so childish. It's common knowledge.'

'What is?' Karen butted in cautiously. I could tell she didn't want to fan the flames but she sounded genuinely puzzled. I was kind of relieved, because I was just about to go for the jugular again.

Mar sighed. 'Don't you read the newspapers? Hear stuff on the TV? They're all the same – all the guys in tourist places like Greece and Turkey and Tunisia. And *Egypt*. Western women are always getting seduced by them.'

'Well . . . maybe. But I'm pretty sure Ali's not like that.' Karen sounded almost as nettled as I felt, and I could have hugged her.

'How do you know he's *not like that*?' Mar's voice rose in outrage. 'We've been here a total of four days. Less. How the f . . .' she slapped her hand against her forehead. 'You just don't get it, do you?'

Karen and I looked at each other. In spite of my defiance, I was close to tears, and that was the last thing I wanted Mar to see.

'Mar,' I said in a low voice. 'One day, you might just look up and notice there's a world out there, with people in it. Not just statistics in a frigging tabloid paper. And maybe, just maybe, you'll end up having fun but I'm not going to hold my breath. Christ, it's not a rut you're stuck in, it's a trench.'

And with that I got up and marched away, before the tears could rise and start spilling over.

Maybe Mar was right. Maybe I was being really stupid and naïve and all the rest of it. The truth is, I wasn't sure; I didn't really know what I was doing with Ali or how I really felt about it. I sat on my bed and squeezed away the tears between my fingers, as Karen came in quietly and shut the door.

'Hey,' she said softly.

She came and sat next to me, then she put her arm

around me, and we sat in silence for a couple of minutes.

'Am I being crazy, Ka?' I asked eventually.

'No,' she said, emphatically. 'Don't listen to her. I mean, I think we still have to be careful, but we're having a brilliant time and Ali's great. If anything had seemed really dodgy, I would have said so.'

I gave her a watery smile. 'Do you mean that?' I asked.

'Of course I mean it,' she said. 'Hey, I wouldn't have missed a minute of it – and I'm not even getting the snogs in.'

'Thanks,' I said. 'It's just . . . I dunno. Mar's never gone off on one like this before. With other people maybe, but never with us. It's like it's . . . it's ruined everything.'

'Yeah. I know. It's like they've become different people, just because we're in a different place.' Karen was silent for a minute. 'But I don't think you should blame yourself,' she carried on eventually. 'Since when did a holiday fling ever hurt anyone? They've just got to deal with it, end of story.'

I frowned. I opened my mouth to speak, then closed it again. The words 'holiday fling' sounded all wrong somehow. I suddenly understood that we were all seeing things from our own perspectives and we'd all got a different idea of what was going on. Karen was having fun, and she thought I was doing the same with a bit of 'action' thrown in. Mar was running scared with tabloid stories galloping around her head – and maybe she was jealous too, like Karen had said. Izzy would always be loyal to her, even if she didn't really agree – but this time, I got the feeling she did.

And me? What did I really think? Karen clearly didn't believe I was taking Ali seriously and that was a bit of a shock. Christ. Did it mean that I *was*? Was I really thinking about him as . . . more? Or was I just playing a game and getting the snogs in, as Karen had put it? I bit my lip. I didn't know.

Karen got up and flopped down on her own bed, then peeled off her trousers to inspect the prickly heat. 'So what are the plans for today then?' she asked. 'My spots are a bit better, but the idea of lying by the pool doesn't fill me with ecstasy.'

I looked at her guiltily. 'Ali asked if I'd go with him to Banana Island.'

'What, in the felucca? Like we did before?'

Karen hadn't twigged. 'Well . . .' I began awkwardly. 'Yeah, in the felucca. But I think he meant . . .' I trailed off. I was terrified of upsetting Karen as well.

The penny dropped. 'Oh. Right.' Karen stared at me. 'So what am I supposed to do with myself all day?'

'We won't be gone all day,' I said hastily. 'I think he just wanted to take me for a trip while it's still quite hot, so he can still fit in some tourists later.'

Karen's face cleared. 'Oh, well, that's OK,' she said. 'I don't mind hanging out here for a couple of hours. I want to finish my book.'

Relief flooded through me. 'You're just the best, Karen,' I said. 'Thanks a million. In fact, thanks for everything. I don't know what I would have done without you.'

Karen grinned. 'Yeah, you owe me, Aston,' she said jokingly.

I hadn't been out on the street on my own before and it was a bit scary. I left the hotel and walked quickly along the Corniche, hoping that the heat of the day would keep everyone subdued. Really, it wasn't too bad. A taxi driver sidled up to me and wound down his window as I walked, but he soon laid off when I ignored him. Then, up ahead, I spotted little Mahmoud in his brown *galabiyya*, and I waved.

'Come. Ali wait,' he said to me.

He led me down to the felucca moorings, and I saw Ali in the *Ali Baba*, sitting on the cushions smoking a Cleopatra. He was gazing over the Nile towards the mountains on the west bank, one lean arm casually flicking ash into the river. His face was serious and I wondered what he was thinking.

Memories of the night before flooded back and for an awful moment I feared he was regretting it. It was pretty obvious that something like that wouldn't happen with an Egyptian girl; I'd hardly seen any my own age, and the ones I had seen certainly weren't hanging out with men. *They haven't got any respect for Western women*, Mar had said. Suddenly I started to worry. How could Ali really respect me when I'd snogged him at the first opportunity?

He looked up and saw me. I held my breath. He stood and beckoned and, as I saw his warm smile creep over his face, I let my breath out in relief. As I got closer, I saw there was a new tenderness in the way he looked at me too. So I hadn't blown it after all . . . I felt that familiar fluttering inside. *Steady, Jen*, I told myself. There was no doubt about it, this guy was getting under my skin.

When we set off up the river, I realised he was nervous. It was like something had changed between us, something important, and that made me nervous too. It was difficult to talk straight away, because Mahmoud had come along to help with the felucca. I saw now that Ali had a close bond with his cousin. He was in cahoots, this little guy, and once again I realised that this had probably happened before. They had it all worked out, this trip up to Banana Island in the heat of the day when most people were flat out in the shade. And what was wrong with that? Like Karen had said, holiday flings never hurt anyone and Ali had probably had a fair few of them, except it was never a holiday for him.

Somehow the thought was depressing and I stayed quiet, watching while Ali made us some *shai* on the little burner. It seemed crazy, drinking hot *shai* when it was forty-five degrees Celcius in the shade, but oddly it did the trick. Maybe by making yourself hotter on the inside it made the outside seem cooler.

Once the *shai* was made, I lounged on the cushions as we sailed gently up the river. As we began to pull in towards Banana Island, Ali and I exchanged glances and I felt a swell of happiness rising up inside me. He took my hand and steadied me as the boat rocked in the shallows, and I leaped for the bank. Mahmoud stayed behind to guard the felucca. We were alone.

The plantation seemed deserted, and no one came to meet us as they had done last time. Ali led me off the main path and through the trees until we came to a gently sloping bank. We slid down it, then stopped where it levelled out above the water's edge. Even if someone had come along the path, they wouldn't have seen us there, and we were protected in the other direction by the water, which was an inlet that swirled around the side of the plantation away from the main stream of the river. Thankfully, the banana trees gave us shade.

It was almost too hot to kiss – but not quite. In fact, we were so both hungry for it it was frightening. But as we clung to each other on that narrow bank, not caring about the crumbling earth on our clothes or the prospect of someone peering down and seeing us, a little voice in the back of my mind made me hold something back. I didn't know how far to go and I didn't want to overstep it. Whatever was going on, I wanted Ali to take me seriously.

We drew apart, panting in the heat. My top was sodden

with sweat. We lay side by side and he stroked my face, wiping a drop from my forehead.

'*Ya* Jen,' he murmured. 'You happy?'

I nodded. 'Yes,' I replied. 'Very happy. And you, Ali?'

His dark eyes closed for a second, and I reached out to trace the line of his lips with my fingers. He kissed them, then opened his eyes. I felt a lurch, because they were clouded and troubled. 'I am happy . . . now,' he said. 'Here. With you. But in my heart I not happy.'

It wasn't what I wanted to hear and my heart thumped painfully against my ribs. 'Why?' I whispered.

'*Ya* Jen,' he said. 'I see many tourists all the time. You know this.'

'Yes,' I replied, hardly able to speak. All my doubts and questions crowded in. Perhaps he already had a girlfriend somewhere else. In Sweden or France or America. Perhaps he had tons of them.

He took my hand. 'But I never do this before,' he said. 'I tell you the true. Never. Always I think I will marry Egyptian woman, maybe one day when my father's new house is finish.'

I sat up, smoothing my hair back off my face. My mouth felt dry. 'Never?' I repeated. I stared at him. Could it really be true? Even though I wanted to believe everything he told me, I knew I had to keep up my guard – especially as I hadn't felt like this for a long, long time. Maybe ever.

'Believe me, *ya* Jen. And so I am not happy, because I think you make game with me. This just holiday for you, you have nice time with Egyptian man, you go back in England, you forget. This your way, *sah*?'

I was dumbfounded. His eyes searched mine. 'Maybe you have boyfriend, in England,' he said.

'No . . . no! I haven't,' I managed to say. 'I really haven't, Ali.'

'But you have one before?'

I couldn't lie about that. I nodded. 'Yes.'

I was worried. We had all spent so much time wondering what Ali was really like and whether we could trust him. But now he'd turned the tables on me. And what he'd said was true, more or less. I had played with guys. I'd had plenty of flings. He was right; that *was* 'my way'.

I swallowed and took his hand. 'There's no one else now, Ali. Only you.'

He sighed. 'Yes. Until next week,' he said softly. He ran a hand through his hair, and shook his head. 'Always I see what happen here, in Luxor. Always I say to myself, I never go with European girl, this bad way, this make problem for me. But what I do. What I do?'

He gazed at me, his face full of dismay, but I could see he wanted me too. He leaned forward and kissed me again, harder than before. He was full of anger – I could feel it. Then we pushed apart and his eyes were flashing.

'What you do now, *ya* Jen?' he demanded. 'You go back

in England and you say you meet Muslim man in Egypt? You say this to your family? What you say?'

I was shaken. I let my breath out slowly. 'Let me think,' I said, in a low voice. 'Please, Ali, let me think.'

He stood up abruptly and scrambled back up the bank, reaching in his pocket for his cigarettes. I stayed where I was for a moment, hugging my knees.

The journey back to Luxor was quiet. Ali had calmed down, and he said that of course, I must think. When Mahmoud had the felucca under safe control, Ali sat next to me on the cushions, his knee touching mine. He smoked while I watched black and white kingfishers diving for their catch, and beautiful white egrets stalking in the shallows on the west bank. We saw a horse galloping full pelt along a track with an Egyptian guy riding him bareback. Ali waved to him and shouted. The rider shouted back.

'My friend Tariq,' Ali told me briefly.

I nodded and smiled. I didn't trust myself to speak. I knew now that I'd just let this happen without thinking about what it meant. I'd fallen in love with this place and fallen in love with my adventure. What I had to decide now was whether I was really falling in love with Ali.

Karen was just fantastic. She wanted to know the lot – where we'd been and what we'd said and how I really felt. I churned it over and over. The others were out at the Sound and Light show, so we went down to the hotel terrace as the heat began to subside and got ourselves a couple of drinks. The sun set, casting a pink glow over the Nile, and the muezzins started up their call to prayer from the mosques. We ordered more drinks. I'd gone over everything about ten times by now.

Karen sighed. 'It's a pity you don't have more time,' she said, playing with the label on her bottle. 'A fortnight isn't really long enough to be sure of someone.'

I detected a note of caution in her voice. 'It isn't over yet!' I said.

'No. But it soon will be.'

'Don't say that,' I begged her. My heart felt a twist of pain at the mere idea of it.

Karen looked at me with this strange expression. 'God, Jen,' she said quietly. 'I don't think I've ever seen you like this. He's really got to you, hasn't he?'

I didn't reply at first. I looked out over the Nile, reliving those moments on Banana Island. I saw the anger in Ali's face, and the way he looked at me, all torn up and confused. The truth was, Karen knew me better than anyone. She knew how I'd felt about guys in the past, and how I ended up feeling bored. It was like none of them had anything real inside of them – it was all just football practice and iPods and computer games. But Ali . . . he was different. He was real, all right. I thought about all the things he'd said that day, and knew that he saw life for what it really was.

'Well . . .' I admitted. 'As you're asking, I think he has.'

Karen gave a little smile. 'Yeah, well, statement of the totally obvious.' She paused. 'There is something you could do,' she said, after a minute. 'To be honest, I'm surprised you haven't thought of it already. It might not be a good idea, but . . .'

'What?' I stared at her.

Karen shrugged. 'Why don't you talk to Lisa?'

'Lisa?' I stared at her. 'What's she got to do with anything?'

'She's staying in a flat,' said Karen. 'If things keep on going well, maybe you could stay with her for a bit.'

I was still gawping like a goldfish. 'What are you talking about?'

Karen sighed. 'Look. You and Ali need more time together, and we've got the whole of August before we go to uni. Maybe you should stay here and check it out. Get to know Ali properly.'

My mouth dropped open. She was right. This possibility hadn't crossed my mind. It was perfect – a few more weeks to work out what was really going on. 'Do you really think so? Like, do you really think I should?' The idea was so exciting I could hardly think straight.

'Well . . .' Karen hesitated. 'It's just an idea. Don't rush into it – it's a big risk . . .'

I could tell she was trying to get me to slow down and think it through properly, but my mind was already on overdrive. What was there to stop me? I sat back and took a deep breath, things crowding in all at once. My dad was the first thing that popped into my mind. He was bound to try and stop me – we'd fought over just about everything for the last five years, from my choices for GCSE to which way to stack the fridge after a Waitrose run. But I was already here, so there wasn't much he could do about that.

'What about my A-level results?' I mused out loud. They'd be coming out in August and I wasn't sure what would happen after that.

'I think you can phone up for them,' said Karen. 'But listen, Jen, don't just make a snap decision . . .'

I didn't want to listen. My excitement began to take over, but for a few more minutes I tried to stay calm and think of reasons why it couldn't happen. 'How am I going to afford it?' I asked. 'I'll lose my flight back and I won't have much left to live on.'

Karen shook her head ruefully. She knew there was no point in trying to make me backtrack now. Instead, she looked thoughtful. She knew what my dad was like. 'You could speak to your mum,' she suggested. 'Tell her you're getting into the history – all the tombs and temples and stuff. Say you want to stay because you're learning so much.'

I giggled. Like she was going to buy *that*. But all the same, Karen had a point, because I *was* learning. I was exploring a whole new world; I was seeing things I'd never even dreamed about before. I sat chewing my lips for a minute, trying to think why else I shouldn't stay. I couldn't think of anything. I laughed out loud and ordered another drink.

# Chapter Five

Things happened quickly after that. It was weird how it all slotted into place. Lisa's flat had two bedrooms and the woman she was sharing with was going back to Germany the following week. Lisa had been thinking of leaving shortly afterwards, but when I asked about living there, she decided to stay. She was pretty rootless, and at the time I couldn't work out what she was really doing in Luxor.

Then there was my mum. I rang her on my mobile. I knew it would cost a fortune but I reckoned it was too important to matter. I told her that I'd made friends in Luxor and that I was learning tons about Egyptian culture, and that I thought it would be much better to stay on and make the most of it than go back to work in the local supermarket. And, you know, she seemed to take it OK. She was a bit doubtful at first, and asked me lots of questions about Lisa and the flat and stuff, but then she gave in. She'd done a bit of travelling when she was young, so I guess she understood – or at least understood the bits I'd told her – and I didn't feel too guilty, because at least those bits were true. She said she'd put some money in my current account and I got the money out of an ATM. Easy. So easy I couldn't quite believe it had happened.

The others couldn't believe it either. Even Karen. She was a bit worried about me, I could tell, but the difference between her and Mar and Izzy was that she was glad to see me happy. The others thought I'd completely lost it. But by that stage, I didn't care. And when I started getting angry text messages from my dad, I just switched my phone off. I figured my mum would talk him round – there wasn't a lot that *I* could do, was there?

Of course, the person who really couldn't get his head around it was Ali. It took him several days to believe I'd actually done it. When he finally realised I was serious, he went really quiet – so much so that I wondered if he'd just been spinning me a line that day on Banana Island. Maybe this wasn't what he wanted after all. But I needn't have worried. One day, I went to meet him and he had this enormous grin on his face. That was when I knew he'd taken it on board.

In the end, I managed to patch things up with Mar and Izzy, more or less. We'd all continued to meet up for breakfast, but they had steadfastly refused to get involved with all the stuff that Karen and I were up to. They just lazed around or stuck to the standard tours while we met up with Ali or explored on our own. But Karen, like the total angel she is, was determined that we should part on good terms. So she persuaded the others to come over to the west bank on their last day. We took donkeys around the mortuary temples and up to the temple of Hatshepsut with Ali and his cousin Said. It was hysterical – all the donkeys were jostling each other, desperate to race, and Izzy nearly fell off. We killed ourselves laughing.

Karen's determination paid off. Mar and Izzy couldn't really be stiff with me, not after that. We went for *shai* in Ali's home and his little sisters did their peeping trick again, then came in shyly and told us their names – Aisha, Layla and Hasina. They were the three youngest – four, seven and ten. I knew Ali had two teenage sisters too, tucked away in the back of the house somewhere, but I hadn't met them yet. I hoped I would. I'd need some girl friends, once the others had gone.

We went back to the hotel to spend a last evening together, just the four of us. Mar and Izzy had got the hang of the *souq* big-time – Mar had probably haggled the stall-holders out of existence – and they seemed to be taking half of Egypt back home with them. It was a good giggle helping them pack their bags, and it meant that we avoided the big, flashing, Ali-sized issue that was hanging between us. I kind of preferred it that way. But when we said our goodbyes, Izzy said she hoped things would work out. And Mar . . . well, she kind of grinned and said,

'Good luck.' That was it. Just 'Good luck'. But somehow, that was enough.

All the same, it was only when they'd left for the airport that what I'd done began to sink in. I moved into Lisa's flat that morning and I sat on my bed, listening to the noises coming up from the street below – the squeaky beep of a scooter, a woman shouting at her kids, the clip-clop of a distant horse-drawn caleche. I felt very alone. Ali was out in the felucca with a group of tourists, but we'd arranged to meet on the west bank later. I was feeling nervous. *Really* nervous. Quite shaky, in fact.

I got up and wandered around the flat, thinking about the others. They'd probably taken off by now and were heading back to Britain with the baked bean brigade and three dozen hubble-bubble *sheeshas* nestled between people's knees. I was missing Karen already, and my heart beat faster at the thought of what might happen now the others had gone. Would Ali come and stay with me in the flat? Did men here *do* that sort of thing? I didn't know.

To calm my nerves, I thought about the one thing that was certain: Ali was gorgeous. I couldn't believe just how great he was compared to all the guys I'd known before. He was sex on legs, of course – but I'd known almost from the start that it was a lot more than that. It was the way he listened to me and teased me, the way he cared for me and was always checking that I was OK. He was brilliant fun too, always larking about with his mates, rolling around laughing. And I loved the way he was this fit outdoor guy on the one hand, so confident around the felucca or his mate's motorbike or his cousin's donkeys, but this gentle, sweet person on the other, worrying about his mother or his sisters or his dad.

Yeah, I'd fallen for him. Big time.

That night, Ali and I went out for dinner together, just the two of us. It was my idea. We hadn't done anything like that before – he'd never come into the Horizon, or out on the East Bank with me and Karen. We'd always gone to the west bank or down the river in the felucca, and in the evenings we'd hung out on house rooftops with his mates, or in those little cafés that serve *shai* and *sheeshas*. Ali had introduced us to Egyptian fast food – spit-roasted chicken and *kosharee,* a mix of pasta, rice and lentils with spicy tomato sauce and bits of crunchy fried onion on top. It was dirt cheap, tasted brilliant and we never once got sick.

But this was our first night on our own and I wanted it to be special. I'd noticed a nice place not far from the ferry landing on the west bank, just a bit tucked away, with hanging lanterns and a courtyard framed with palm trees. It looked dead romantic and I wanted to buy Ali a treat. It was difficult to work out how poor he really was – I guessed he made a fair amount on the felucca, but he seemed to be supporting most of the family with it, and the family home looked pretty bare to my eyes.

So when I stepped off the ferry that evening, I told Ali what I had planned and he grinned, shaking his head.

'This not place for me, *ya* Jen,' he said.

'Don't be crazy,' I protested. 'This is our first night. It's special. I don't mind paying.'

He looked at me kind of warily. 'But this for tourists . . .' he said. 'Maybe they say . . .' he trailed off.

I looked into his eyes. 'You're with me, Ali,' I said. 'Does it matter what they say?'

He shrugged again, and looked kind of shy. 'Thank you, *ya* Jen,' he said. 'OK. We go.'

I didn't give it another thought after that. I assumed he was just a bit awkward about sitting among a load of Westerners – I couldn't really blame him. Looking back, he seemed quite uncomfortable at first, but the place was quiet and the owner came over and spoke to him. They seemed to know each other, and once he'd taken our order, Ali relaxed. It was a fantastic evening – one of those evenings you remember forever. We sat in the courtyard at a little candlelit table and talked and laughed in the warm night air. We giggled at one of the waiters, who kept shooing away the cats that wandered around scrounging for food. We joked about how we might have a little restaurant of our own one day. I said that Ali could run the restaurant and I'd run the felucca. I'd be the first ever blonde Western felucca captain. And somehow, even though it was all a million miles from anything I ever imagined I do, it all seemed perfectly possible.

Then, when we'd eaten, we shared a *sheesha toffah*, an apple tobacco *sheesha* that tasted delicious and gave me a gentle buzz – not like cigarettes, which make me feel sick, but just warm and fuzzy inside. Perfect. We left, and Ali suggested we take a service taxi part of the way home.

'We stop early, so we walk through the sugarcane,' he said, brushing my hand with his as we walked up the street. 'This good idea?'

I nodded. Yes, it was a good idea. I was beginning to realise that nowhere was private here. Everyone lived on top of each other, and everyone knew everyone else's business. Unless you had your own home, there was little chance of keeping anything a secret. But there were sugarcane fields too.

It was almost a full moon, and so, so quiet in the fields. We headed along a little track in the silvery light, and heard a donkey braying in one of the villages. I was very aware of Ali close by my side, his *galabiyya* swishing gently as he walked. We stopped. We looked at each other, breathing quickly. I remember thinking that Ali's face, sculpted by the moonlight, was the most deeply, wildly gorgeous face I'd ever seen. And then, almost in slow motion, we leaned towards each other. And kissed.

I don't know how long we stood there. Ali moved his lips slowly over my face, kissing my forehead, my eyelids, my lips with one hand caressing the back of my neck and fondling my hair.

'You so beautiful, ya Jen,' he murmured into my ear. 'I never think I meet woman like you.'

I pulled him closer to me and we began to kiss harder, more urgently, his tongue entwining with mine.

'Come back with me,' I said eventually, looking into his eyes. 'Come back to Lisa's flat.'

Ali pulled away slightly and grew still. 'This not possible,' he said softly.

My heart thudded painfully in my chest. I knew he wanted me – wanted more. And God knows I did. But at the same time I was scared, because I still hadn't worked out how things happened here. Again, I compared myself to Egyptian girls. I was sure you wouldn't catch them out snogging in the sugarcane fields. No way. But Ali knew we did things differently in England and he seemed to accept me for who I was.

'Why not?' I asked tentatively.

Ali stroked my hair, and said nothing for a few moments. 'Better we wait, *ya* Jen,' he said eventually. 'I think maybe Lisa not like this.'

'*Lisa?*' I was gobsmacked. 'What's she got to do with it? You don't know her.'

Ali gave a low chuckle. 'I know her, *ya* Jen. Everybody know her.' He paused, his black eyebrows folding into a frown. 'Everybody know *you* also. You know this?'

It wasn't quite what I'd meant, but I could see what he was saying. It was pretty obvious. Westerners stood out, and gossip spread like wildfire. And standing there under the stars, with the sugarcane rustling in the warm breeze and Ali's thigh pressed against mine, I suddenly didn't mind keeping things low-key. In England I'd always felt under so much pressure with guys. Here, I felt different, and it was kind of refreshing.

I nodded. 'I know. It's OK, Ali. It's good.' I thought of our conversation on Banana Island, and mimicked him. *'This your way.'*

Ali smiled. He looked pleased, and nodded. 'My way,' he repeated, and folded his arms around me.

The days began to slip by, fantastic golden days full of love and new discoveries. I found out that Ali could ride, so we hired horses from the Pharaoh's stables and rode out into the desert, skirting around the magnificent temple of Ramesses III at Medinet Habu and galloping through the dunes beyond under the shadow of the mountain, or riding through the fields and little villages closer to the Nile, cantering along tracks lined with date palms, passing the odd tethered donkey or water buffalo. I loved watching Ali's straight back as he rode along, the sun glinting on his golden skin, and I loved the way he rode one-handed, with the other lying gently on his horse's neck.

We spent hours lounging in the felucca too, messing around. Ali was trying to teach me Arabic. Every day, he taught me a few more words and killed himself laughing at my pronunciation. But I was getting there. I grew to love the way he started sentences with *yani*, just like we say 'well,' or 'you know . . .', without even noticing. I knew *habibi*, my darling; *kwayis*, good; *momkin*, possible and *jameel*, beautiful. I knew the numbers up to ten; *iwa,* yes; *la,* no; how to say hello and how to ask questions – how, where and why. And of course, I knew *insh'allah*, which they all said all the time – *God willing*.

Once a week, I rose early and went to meet Ali's mother. To my surprise, she'd taken to me, a Western girl, dating her only son. I'd somehow expected her to have more of a problem with it, but if she did, she never showed it. Through Ali, she had offered to take me around the weekly *souq* on the west bank – not a tourist *souq* but the real market for locals where they bought their groceries, meat and even clothes. Walking around it was fantastic fun, a total buzz – it was so full of life and colour with huge mounds of fruit and veg lying around, and everyone taking their business very seriously. It was pretty obvious that this was the women's domain. I'd never seen so many local women anywhere else, but on market day they all came out dressed in their respectable black to get the family shopping and exchange gossip.

We had to get there by service taxi, because the market was further north, beyond the road that led to the Valley of the Kings, on a patch of land by the temple of Seti I. With

Chapter Five

Ali's mum not speaking English and me not speaking Arabic, it was sign language all the way, but we managed, pointing, laughing and nodding. Ali's Arabic lessons helped. I was a bit shocked when I realised that buying meat meant buying a live chicken and carrying it back with us in the service taxi, along with a dozen other women and their squawking birds. And it felt even weirder to go round to Ali's house later, knowing I'd have to eat the poor thing. But it was all part of being there and part of feeling accepted.

But then one week I showed up in the morning and Ali's mother couldn't come. The oldest daughter Jameela was going to the market instead. She was about my age but really shy; I'd soon worked out that we wouldn't be mates, even if we'd been able to talk to each other properly. It was kind of disappointing. But anyway, when we got back, I asked Ali if his mum was OK.

'Yes, she fine,' he told me. He shrugged awkwardly. 'Just they make the cut for Layla yesterday. My mother stay with her.'

I stared at him, not understanding. I knew Layla was the seven year old, but I had no idea what he was talking about.

'You mean she's had an accident?'

'No, no, not accident. The doctor come and do this. Everything OK.' Ali ran his hand through his hair. He frowned as he looked at me. 'Maybe this not happen in England,' he said.

I didn't know either way, and Ali wouldn't explain – or couldn't. I wasn't sure.

It wasn't until the next day that I found out what he was talking about. I didn't see much of Lisa, but sometimes we went to the pool at the Horizon for a swim, and we'd decided to go there that morning. I still hadn't sussed her. I knew she was twenty-two, and that she'd come to Luxor with her parents a few times in her early teens. She knew a lot of guys on either side of the river but she never had any of them back to the flat. It wasn't really like she was on holiday; she seemed to know the place too well somehow.

Anyway, we went down to the pool, and spread ourselves on a couple of loungers. I was slapping on the suncream when I remembered what Ali had said.

'What do you think he meant?' I asked.

Lisa shrugged. 'Circumcision, I guess,' she said briefly.

My mouth dropped open. 'What . . . you mean . . .' I frowned. 'But . . . Layla's a girl.'

Another shrug. 'All the women here are circumcised. Well, nearly all. Someone told me ninety-seven per cent are. You didn't know?'

'Ninety-sev . . .' I gulped. I shook my head, still barely able to take it in. I wasn't even fully sure what it meant. I'd guess I'd heard about stuff like that on the news but I'd never really thought about it. I looked at Lisa awkwardly. 'But what do they actually *do*?' I asked.

'They cut off the clitoris,' said Lisa matter-of-factly. 'Sometimes just the top. Sometimes more.'

I winced and instinctively plaited my legs. I couldn't believe that all the women I'd met – Ali's mum and all his sisters, all the women I passed on the street – had gone through this. It seemed incredible.

'But . . .' I couldn't get my head around it. 'Do they *want* it done? Can't they stop it?'

'Sure they want it. They think it makes women clean.' Lisa laid her head on her hands and closed her eyes.

I lapsed into silence, my thoughts in turmoil. I couldn't believe that someone like Ali really approved of it. How? *How?* And if they thought it made women clean, where did that leave me? Was I dirty because I hadn't had it done? I had more questions but Lisa had turned her head away, so I thought it through on my own. If they chopped off the clitoris, it must stop women from enjoying themselves. And that must be why they did it, not to be clean. Maybe that was just what people said to justify it. Christ.

Lisa's voice broke into my thoughts. 'They say here that it's a Muslim thing but it isn't really,' she said lazily. 'It happened before Islam came along. And anyway lots of Muslim countries manage fine without it – Saudi Arabia and Iran and places like that.' She rolled over and looked at me. 'I tell you something else. Less than half of the women here can read and write. This is a poor country, Jen.'

I stared at her. 'How do you know this stuff?' I asked her. Then I realised it was the wrong question. '*Why* do you know? What are you really doing here?'

Lisa sat bolt upright, very suddenly, swung her legs over the side of the lounger and stood up. 'I am here because I want to understand,' she snapped. 'Isn't it obvious?'

And with that, she dived into the pool.

No, it wasn't obvious. In fact, the more time I spent in Luxor, the more problems I had finding anything that was obvious, apart from Ali himself.

That afternoon, he borrowed a friend's motorbike and we drove out into the desert, bumping over white gravelly tracks out to the west, my hair streaming out behind us. I leaned my chin on Ali's shoulder as the wind whipped my eyes and Ali skewed the bike this way and that.

'I take you to see the church!' he shouted over the noise.

'The what?' I wasn't sure I'd heard right.

'The place for the Christians,' he said.

I didn't know what he meant so I decided to wait and see. It turned out to be a monastery, out in the middle of nowhere – a really ancient one that dated from the third century or something crazy. I had a wander around while Ali waited outside; for some reason, he felt shy about entering himself. I'd noticed that about other places too, like the tombs and the temples. You never saw Egyptians wandering around them, or at least, you never saw locals, unless they worked there. Too expensive, I suppose. But I think Ali was awkward at the monastery because it was Christian, and that made me curious.

'Are the people who work here Christian?' I asked him, as we clambered back on to the bike again. There had been quite a few women but they dressed just like Muslims as far as I could tell, though a couple of them looked more like nuns.

'Of course,' said Ali, looking surprised.

'So there are Egyptian Christians?'

'Yes, yes,' said Ali. 'These people Copts. You not know this name?'

I shook my head.

'Many Copts in Luxor,' said Ali. He paused. '*Yani*, not many, many. Some.'

'And how can you tell which ones are Copts?' I asked, feeling a bit dumb.

Ali shrugged. 'Look same, like Muslim people. I have some friends Copts.' He turned to look at me and grinned. 'This make you happy, *ya* Jen?'

I laughed. 'I don't mind either way. It's interesting, though.'

'You not mind? You like to be Muslim?' Ali hadn't started the bike up yet, and he was obviously interested to hear what I'd say.

I didn't know how to answer. In the end, I hedged it. 'I'm just myself,' I said. 'Not Christian, not Muslim. Just Jen.'

Ali laughed, and I felt relieved. 'This good answer, *ya* Jen,' he said.

'Well . . . I hope so,' I said. Suddenly I felt anxious. 'But I know things are different here. Lisa told me about Layla. About the cutting. We don't do this in England.'

Ali shifted his weight uneasily on the motorbike seat, and put his hands over mine, which were already resting around his waist. 'This problem for you?' he asked quietly.

I hesitated. I felt afraid. I didn't want anything like this to come between us – stuff about us being from different cultures and different religions. 'I don't like it,' I admitted eventually. I smiled. 'But this your way.'

Ali looked thoughtful. 'Maybe not my way,' he said. 'Maybe I sometimes different. I think about this, many times, in the night when I not sleep. I think about how I now with European girl.' He frowned. 'We must go little bit my way, little bit your way. If we not do this, we have big problem, *sah*?'

I squeezed his waist. It was such a fantastic thing for him to say and I felt relief wash over me. 'Thank you, Ali,' I whispered. 'You're right. *Sah*.'

# Chapter Six

Thursday 18th August was just like any other day in Luxor. I'd almost forgotten what day it was back home, but not quite. It was the day our A-level results came out and the truth was I didn't want to have to think about it. But I did ring home, all the same, and got the news from my mum. Turned out I'd done OK – two As and a C – but not quite as well as I'd hoped. The C in history of art was a bit of a bummer, as it meant that my first two choices – Durham and Bristol – wouldn't accept me. But my English teacher had told me that my third choice, Sheffield, was a good place to do English. So that was it. I'd be going to Sheffield.

*Sheffield*. It didn't seem real. I found Ali on the Corniche, chatting to a couple of the touts. He jogged up to me, his face alight with concern.

'You do well in your exam?' he asked me.

I shrugged, and smiled. 'Well enough,' I told him. I

didn't want to talk about it. I didn't want to think about leaving Egypt.

We began to walk along the Corniche together, and went to sit in the *Ali Baba*. Ali lit a cigarette. 'You go in the university?' he asked me.

'I guess so,' I said.

We were both silent for a couple of minutes. I could sense that Ali was thinking hard.

'You come back, *ya* Jen?' he said eventually, his voice soft.

It was weird, like he didn't really know what to expect. And he was right, because I didn't know how I was going to feel when I got home. At that moment, I just couldn't imagine being in England, studying again, seeing my mates, going down the pub, and out to clubs on a Saturday night.

So I said what I wanted to believe. 'Of course I'll come back, Ali.'

We looked at each other then. Ali's eyes were big and full of anxiety. '*Insh'allah*,' he said, his voice cracking slightly. 'I hope.'

I took a deep breath. I knew I had to take the plunge, whatever happened when I got back. It just wasn't fair otherwise. 'I'll come back. I promise.'

Ali reached over and touched my hand. 'I love you, *ya* Jen,' he said.

It was the first time he'd said it. I let the words hang in the air between us like an invisible thread. I didn't want to spoil the moment by saying the same in return, not just then. I wanted to wait for the right moment. So I just squeezed his hand, and blinked away two little tears.

The first time I told Ali I loved him was two days later, after a glorious ride out to the desert on horseback. It was quite scary, saying those words, because I realised that I really meant it. I was only eighteen, and I'd always thought I'd meet the love of my life when I was older. But I guess life's just not like that.

After that, it was like time began to speed up. Before my A-level results, it had seemed like we had forever – weeks and weeks of glorious happy adventures in the sun and all the time in the world to get to know each other. But now, with my mum having made me promise I'd be home by early September, the days seemed like gold dust. We savoured each one, but even so they slipped through our fingers like water. We began to count the sunsets. Only ten left. We counted my trips to the market. Just two to go. We counted everything – our walks in the sugarcane fields, the *sheesha toffahs*, our riding expeditions, the number of days we had to laze around in the felucca. And soon there was only one of everything left and I was packing my bags in Lisa's flat.

'I don't know what I do without you.' Ali was sitting on my bed while I stuffed shirts and trousers into my rucksack, blindly. They were all crumpled and I just didn't care. I couldn't answer.

He hadn't been to the flat before. It had been like an unspoken deal between us, ever since that walk in the sugarcane fields after the others had left. Now that he was sitting there surrounded by my stuff, it felt like he was out of place. This was my little world and he wasn't part of it. It was an awful feeling, because I knew it was only going to get worse. I was going back to somewhere that he'd never seen and couldn't understand. I didn't want to go.

'I'll come back.' I managed to croak the words out, my throat constricted with tears. 'I promise, Ali. I'll come back.'

Ali stood up, his eyes dark with emotion, and pulled me roughly towards him. I broke down then and sobbed on his shoulder. He rocked me and stroked my hair. It was only when we moved apart so I could reach for a tissue to blow my nose that I saw his face and realised he was crying too.

Ali had arranged for his uncle Tayib to take me to the airport. Tayib would drive all the way around from the west bank to reach the centre of Luxor, via the bridge to the south, and I wasn't very impressed with his 'special price'. But I'd got used to the idea that most of Ali's extended family didn't like giving me favours. If anything, they thought it should be the other way round and maybe they were right.

By this stage, I didn't care. All I could think about was

how I was going to feel when I got on that plane with a load of British holiday-makers. Like shit.

It just seemed like that day got worse and worse. I couldn't believe what a palaver we had getting to the airport. It was the last thing we needed, it really was. There were these military guys who stopped the car on the outskirts of Luxor and made us get out. Once they'd seen my passport they lost interest in me, but for some reason, they quizzed Ali and Tayib until the cows came home. They looked through their papers so many times I thought I was going to miss the plane.

'What was all that about?' I asked Ali, when they eventually got back into the car.

Both he and his uncle seemed pretty flustered. 'Bad government,' muttered Ali. 'Don't worry, *ya* Jen.' Then he hesitated, and turned around to look at me, his eyes wide and a little frightened. 'Better I not touch you in the airport. We say goodbye in the car. OK?'

I didn't know what to say. I didn't want our parting to be spoiled by . . . by what? I didn't even know what was going on. I just nodded, my heart like lead. 'Fine,' I whispered. 'Everything's fine, Ali.'

It didn't feel fine though. It felt all wrong to stand apart from him on the airport tarmac, my rucksack on my shoulder, surrounded by tour buses and taxis and police. Suddenly, Ali seemed young and small, younger than myself, even though he was three years older. I was leaving him. I didn't want to but that's the way it was. I was the one going back to my own world where he couldn't imagine me, and I knew that was why he looked so vulnerable. He held his hand up in farewell, just held it there, as though it was stuck in mid-air. I couldn't bear it for long. I waved, turned around, and walked into the terminal.

Gatwick airport on a cold September night. Well, it probably wasn't that cold, but after summer in Luxor anywhere would feel freezing. I waited for my rucksack to come round on the luggage carousel, not knowing what to feel. I knew that part of me was going to be glad to see Mum and Dad and Toby, my sixteen-year-old brother. Another part of me was dreading it. I had no idea how Dad was going to react to me. Let's face it, we fought about everything and judging by the tone of the texts he'd sent me, I feared the worst.

But whatever he felt, he was obviously under strict instructions from Mum to keep a lid on it at the airport. As I walked through duty free and out through the exit, I saw their three faces peering for me anxiously and I suddenly felt really emotional. I ran to Mum and she gave me this enormous hug.

'I'm so pleased to see you, sweetheart,' she whispered into my ear. It was too much. For the second time that day, I burst into tears on someone's shoulder.

Toby punched my arm while I mopped my eyes and

sniffed, and my Dad gave me a kind of lop-sided grin.

'Good to have you back,' said Dad. I should have known then that this was as good as it was going to get, but I was feeling too wobbly to realise it at the time.

The normality of the drive back home was a major culture shock. Toby sat in the back seat next to me, listening to his iPod the whole way, which really pissed me off. Not that we had to talk about Egypt loads or anything, but a *bit* of interest would have been nice. Not one iota. Not from Toby. Not even from Mum and Dad. Dad just drove like he always did – burning away from the traffic lights like some overgrown kid. And Mum gave me all the gossip, non-stop. First all the stuff she'd heard about my friends from school – Eloise from down the road had done unexpectedly well in her A-levels so she was going to take a gap year and apply to Oxford . . . Ian Jones had been in a car crash and was OK, but had written off the car he'd been given for his eighteenth birthday . . . Then she moved on to all the gossip from the deli that she and Dad ran in town, followed by the low-down on all the relatives. Honestly, you'd have thought I'd been away for eight years, not eight weeks, though in another way it was like I'd been nowhere at all. It was like Egypt didn't exist.

It all made me feel wretched and miserable and I was already desperately missing Ali. After being so glad to see my family waiting for me, by the time we got home, all I wanted to do was escape.

\* \* \*

It wasn't until the next day that the penny really dropped. All that cheerful claustrophobic chatter from Mum, all that careful skirting around the E word, had been for one very simple reason. She was trying to keep the peace. Trying to pretend everything was OK. And it wasn't. God, it so wasn't.

Dad collared me at breakfast. It was a Sunday morning. Toby was out with his mates and Mum had just popped out to take something round to a neighbour. I was feeling a bit lost, looking over the cereal packets and trying to decide what to eat. Trouble was, I wasn't hungry. All I could think of were the breakfasts I'd eaten with Ali on the west bank. It had become completely normal to sit together at nine in the morning eating *fuul* and *taamiya* – mashed fava beans and little balls a bit like the falafels we get here, only lighter and tastier and fresh green inside, with pitta bread, salad and pickled vegetables. And hot *shai* to wash it down afterwards. The guys on the west bank had got used to me; they didn't hassle or pass comment. They just served me like a regular customer.

I must have sighed or something, because Dad looked up from the papers.

'You're back, Jen,' he said. 'No good sighing. And if I'd had my way, you'd have been back a lot sooner. Anything could have happened to you out there.'

I'd picked up the packet of Sugarpuffs and now I held it,

suspended, in mid-air, wondering what was coming next.

'At least we've got you back safe. It's a good job you're off to Sheffield in a couple of weeks,' Dad carried on. 'Give you a chance to forget all this nonsense.'

I banged the cereal box down on the kitchen table. 'It's not nonsense,' I snapped.

Dad shook his paper, and folded it back on itself. 'Oh, I suppose you think you'll be going back out there, do you?'

I suddenly realised that they had worked it out. They hadn't been fooled by all that 'Egyptian culture' stuff. Or maybe Mum had been fooled when I spoke to her, but Dad had soon set her right. I said nothing, my mind working overtime. I turned away and fetched myself a bowl, a spoon and some milk from the fridge.

'So what's his name?'

I could feel my anger building up. Why did Dad *always* have to get at me like this? 'Who?' I snapped.

Dad snorted. 'Nice try, Jen.'

'It's none of your business.' I knew it sounded childish, but that was the effect Dad had on me. 'I'm eighteen. I can do what I like.'

Dad flung his paper down on the table. 'None of my business? Well, I think you'll find, Jen Aston, that anything that affects the family purse-strings *is* my business.'

'It wasn't you who sent me the money. It was Mum.'

'I'm *very much aware* of who sent you the money, Jen.'

He said it slowly, deliberately, and that was when I realised that Mum and Dad must have been at each others' throats over this. We heard a click. The front door opened and shut. Then Mum stood in the kitchen doorway, looking at us warily, like either of us might explode.

'We're having a little chat,' said Dad, in this horrible snidey tone. 'About Jen's finances.'

Mum stiffened. She raised her eyebrows. Then she took off her jacket and started to fill the kettle from the tap. 'It's all over now,' she said briskly. 'The money's spent. There's no point in arguing about it.'

'Who said we were arguing?' asked Dad. He loved doing this – goading everyone, making himself sound all innocent and reasonable when *he* was the one causing all the trouble in the first place.

My Mum paused. 'I didn't,' she said eventually. 'And I'd rather you didn't start.'

'Oh, I see!' exclaimed Dad. 'Let's just send money out to our wayward daughter, let her gallivant off with some Mohammed or other, then brush the whole thing under the carpet, sell the spare car to cover the costs and forget that anything ever happened. Bloody marvellous.'

That did it. 'He isn't "some Mohammed or other",' I shouted. 'His name's Ali and he's better than all the men in England put together. He's not racist, for a start!'

'Jen!' Mum sounded shocked. 'Don't accuse your father of that.'

'Well, he shouldn't be so pigheaded!' I cried. 'He doesn't know anything about it or anything about people in Egypt. Ali's family accepted me for who I was, so why can't Dad accept Ali? He's just an ign—'

'That's enough.' Mum stopped me with one of her looks. She turned to my dad. 'We didn't sell the spare car, Colin. It was money we could easily afford. Don't provoke her.'

Dad grunted and picked up the paper again. Typical. He'd get us all boiling mad and then just pull the plug on the argument, just when it was getting going and nothing had been resolved. It was so, so infuriating. I ran out of the kitchen, slamming the door behind me.

I was staring out of my bedroom window when Mum knocked on the door. There were a couple of squirrels chasing each other around the sycamore at the end of the garden, and I was just kind of looking at them without really watching. It had just started to rain.

'Come in,' I said dully.

Mum opened the door. I suddenly felt close to tears. This was all so different from the way I'd been welcomed by Ali's family. I turned around, slumped on the bed and let them flow. Mum sat down next to me and stroked my shoulder, then handed me a tissue.

'Why is it always like this, Mum?' I asked, blowing my nose. 'He just . . . *kills* me.'

'He doesn't mean to.'

'Yeah, right.'

'He doesn't. Jen, you're his little girl. He can't stand the idea of anything happening to you, that's all. I know he doesn't express it very well . . .'

'You bet he doesn't.'

Mum cleared her throat. 'You have to believe that we worry about you, Jen.'

'*We?* I thought you were on my side.' I looked at Mum indignantly. 'You sent me the money.'

'Yes. But you weren't completely honest with me, were you?' Mum's voice was ever so slightly sharp and I caught a flash of resentment in her eyes. 'You didn't tell me you were seeing someone. Mind you, it wasn't difficult to work out.'

'OK. So I was seeing someone. I *am* seeing someone.' I crumpled up the tissue and threw it into my bin. I was beginning to feel really miserable now. 'And what, exactly, is wrong with that?'

Mum didn't reply. She hesitated. 'You said his name's Ali,' she said, in a gentler tone.

I nodded.

'And he lives in Luxor?'

I nodded again. 'He's got a felucca. It's like a sail boat that goes on the Nile.'

'Sounds lovely.' Mum seemed to be very conciliatory all of a sudden, and I wasn't sure whether to be suspicious. 'And that's how he makes his living?'

'Yes. It's actually his dad's felucca but Ali does the work now.'

'I see.'

I got the sense that Mum was groping for words that wouldn't upset me, and I wished she wouldn't. 'Look,' I said. 'I'm eighteen. It's up to me who I go out with.'

Mum drew in her breath. 'Can I ask you a question?'

'Sure.'

'How do you think you will keep this going?' She looked at me. 'You *are* thinking of keeping it going, I take it.'

I shrugged. 'I'll go out there in the holidays. Maybe he could come here.' I hated the way it sounded, sitting in my bedroom back in grey September England. When I'd been in Luxor, everything had seemed possible, but now it just sounded like a fantasy. That was how my mum saw it, I could tell. But it wasn't, I reminded myself. It was real. Ali was real. Our love for each other was real.

'And what will you do for money?' asked Mum.

I looked at her quickly. I knew from the way she asked that I wouldn't be getting any more from her. There was only so much she'd do that would annoy Dad; she was always loyal to him in the end.

I stood up, and started pulling dirty clothes out of my rucksack. 'I'll use Aunt Carrie's fund,' I said.

To be honest, the idea had only occurred to me on the spur of the moment. Aunt Carrie was actually a great-aunt on my mum's side. She'd never had children and

Mum had always been her favourite niece, so she'd been tucking away money into funds for me and Toby for years. Not much, but it had built up. Then, when she'd died a couple of years ago, she'd said in her will that we could have the money when we reached eighteen. I'd always thought I'd hold on to it and use it later to help me buy a car or a flat or something. Well, that's what Mum had always suggested and I'd just gone along with it. Until now.

I glanced at my Mum and saw that she'd gone a bit pale. 'You can't do that,' she said.

'Why not?'

Mum looked upset. 'Well . . . you can. I can't stop you. But don't. Please – just don't.'

Suddenly, I thought of Ali, standing waving me goodbye in the airport. I thought of his gorgeous soft eyes and his black hair glistening in the sun. My heart turned a somersault. I folded my arms and stared at Mum.

'You think this is a waste, don't you?' I said bitterly. 'The one time I meet a guy who's everything I ever dreamed of, you and Dad don't want to know. You've got all your set ideas about what it's like out there and the truth is, you're worried because he's a Muslim.'

'Jen – that's not true . . .'

'Well that's how it sounds.'

'We–' She corrected herself. 'I just think you'll end up getting hurt. However nice he is, he's thousands of miles away and from a completely different culture. It can't possibly last, sweetheart.'

It was hard, hearing that from my Mum. She usually spoke sense – more or less. She'd let me get away with a lot too – nights out 'staying with friends', weekends away. I wouldn't have had half as much freedom if it wasn't for her, and I knew that deep down, in spite of what I'd said, that she would never be prejudiced just because of where someone came from.

I carried on unpacking my stuff and picked up a white shirt that had a mark down the front. My mind flashed back to how it had happened. Ali and I had been riding and when we'd got back I'd hugged my beautiful Arabian mare. She'd nuzzled me affectionately and slobbered all over my shirt. We'd laughed and Ali had pretended to tell the mare off. And that's when I'd told him I loved him.

I felt tears welling up again, and swallowed them back. 'I love him, Mum,' I said. 'Isn't that enough?'

Mum said nothing. She studied her hands, and played with a chip in her nail varnish. 'I can't answer that question, Jen,' she said, eventually. 'Sometimes it is. Sometimes it isn't.' She sighed and gave a resigned shrug. 'Well, you'll be off to Sheffield soon.'

As though she, like Dad, thought that would somehow help matters.

# Chapter Seven

I hated Sheffield from Day One. I had a feeling I would, but it was even worse than I'd been expecting: grey, cold and wet with a city centre that seemed to be one big tower block, famous only for stainless steel cutlery and *The Full Monty*. Huh. Says it all really. But if I'm honest I think I would have hated wherever I'd gone. Being back in England, back to studying, back to the same old, same old – it just wasn't where I was at. Let's face it, my heart was still in Luxor.

The others – Karen, Mar and Izzy – had all stayed down south. Mar and Izzy were going into London – Izzy to LSE and Marianne to Queen Mary's – and Karen was off to Sussex Uni in Brighton. It had been hard, saying goodbye. They were all full of excitement at the prospect of a new life, whereas my insides felt like lead. I guess I felt stranded, heading up north. And what was totally, utterly hideous was that I discovered I'd have to share a room.

I was living in halls, Sorby Hall of Residence to be

precise – the oldest-looking hall and the shabbiest. The rooms were along gloomy corridors with a smelly utility room and a shared shower block at one end. Most of the rooms were single, but by some shattering stroke of bad luck I was in an end room that had a cramped 'study area' with two minuscule bedrooms leading off it.

Mum and Dad had driven me up with all my stuff and even they were a bit shocked. Not shocked enough to complain or get me out of there, mind. I guess they took it for granted that student accommodation was basic, used year-in, year-out by freshers and designed to be character-building. And in any case, after two and a half weeks of a barely maintained truce with my dad, I wasn't due any favours. They left pretty quickly, leaving me to wonder what my wonderful room-mate was going to be like.

I didn't have to wait long to find out. I heard her before I saw her, shrieking her head off along the corridor. *Fantastic*, I thought, as an enormous yukka plant barged in through the door, with an even larger person carrying it.

'Hey, room-mate,' she said, giving me a horsey grin. 'I'm Shell.'

She dumped the yukka in the middle of the so-called study area as another person followed her in. I did a double take. She was identical to Shell, and for one sickening moment I thought I'd have to share with both of them.

'This is my twin, Manda,' said Shell. She must have seen

my expression. 'Don't worry,' she added. 'Manda's not staying. She's the thick one.'

They both howled with laughter. I stared at them in shock – two monsters, both about six foot two and built like rugby players with voices to match. What had I done to deserve this?

'Hi,' I managed to say faintly. 'I'm Jen.'

The next two or three days were a queue-filled blur. Registration, sorting out tuition fees, a health check, you name it – all involved standing around in the Octagon or the sports centre, listening to other students discussing their A-level results. The one small mercy was that my surname begins with A, so I got it all over with relatively quickly.

I wandered around campus trying to get my bearings. It was easy to spot fellow freshers because we all had these bright yellow folders filled with the necessary bumpf, which made me feel about six years old. No one else seemed to mind. They were all too busy fooling around on the paternoster lifts in the Arts Tower, or seeing how many shots of tequila they could down in one sitting.

That was the other thing. Everyone else was drinking for England, but I couldn't see the point. I went to the Leadmill and Kingdom club nights and all the rest of it, but my heart wasn't in it. I'd speak to Ali on the phone every few days and I could hardly bring myself to describe all the stuff that went on. It was a million miles from the way he lived and I knew he'd just hate it. Unlike my lovely room-mate Shell. It soon became clear that appearances were not deceptive. She *was* a rugby player. Women's rugby was her thing – that, male rugby players and about fifteen pints of lager a night.

I wandered around the Freshers' Fair in a dream. Every other person seemed to be in some kind of frenzy, as though their entire life depended on me joining the Extreme Sports Society or the Young Conservatives or the Archery Club. By the time I left, my bag was bulging with leaflets and my head was ready to burst. All the other freshers were networking furiously but I went back to my room on my own and flung myself down on my bed.

Christ. Was this really what being a student was all about? Everyone was so . . . *eager*. In an odd sort of way, it reminded me of those guys on the Corniche in Luxor, hounding tourists and begging for scraps. I was beyond all that now; I had Ali and a whole other life. But all the same, part of me was scared. I knew the score. If I didn't play the game, I'd be left out in the cold, and being here would only get worse.

I began to live for my phone calls to Ali. He couldn't afford to call me, and it was too expensive for me to use my mobile. And of course we couldn't use e-mail, as Ali only knew the Arabic script. So I had to buy these 'Dog 'n' Bone' phonecards for ten pounds each and use the payphone on the hall corridor. *Payphone.* Christ, when did anyone last use one of those? It was horrible, standing there, thinking of Ali fishing his mobile out of his *galabiyya* pocket in the warm Egyptian evenings, trying to make sense of this hell-hole I'd landed in. But it was all we had and every last word we shared was precious.

'*Ya* Jen, I miss you too much,' he said one night, his voice forlorn and distant.

'I know. I hate it here,' I told him. 'I wish I was still in Luxor with you.'

There was a pause on the other end of the line. 'You come back soon?' Ali asked eventually. I could hear the hope in his voice.

'I can't yet. Not until the end of term.'

I'd explained how our terms worked, but he kept on asking me when I was going back. I guessed it was because he was afraid I wouldn't. It must have been really hard for him, trying to imagine my life as a student and he must have wondered if it would take me away from him. I knew that's how I would have felt in his position.

'You let me know when you come, *ya* Jen.' His voice was rough, and I could almost feel his disappointment. My heart ached. I didn't know what to say.

Just then, a bunch of other freshers came through the door – blokes singing some god-awful rugby song. New mates of Shell's, I guessed. It was only seven o'clock in the evening and they were already pissed. When they saw me, they grinned like idiots, and one of them grabbed his crotch and thrust his hips in my direction. I gave them a look of pure disgust, then realised that Ali was saying something.

'What happen, *ya* Jen?' I heard.

'Nothing. It's just some wankers,' I said. Literally, I thought to myself.

'What is this? Wan . . . ?'

I sighed. 'Just some guys. Don't worry, Ali.'

It was so crap. How could I explain what really happened in the first term at an English university? I wasn't even sure I wanted to. He didn't need to know – it would only confirm his worst fears about life in the West. And yet I felt uncomfortable, because deep down I knew that if it wasn't for him, I'd probably be out there living it up with the rest of them. We said our goodbyes, and I hung up.

I didn't want to go back to my room, not with Shell and her rugby mates crowded in there. Everyone else was gearing up for another night of major boozing, and I just felt wretched that I didn't want to, but I couldn't be with Ali either. I walked down from Sorby Hall towards the University campus and decided to ride the trams. I don't know why I did that. It was just an escape I guess. I bought a Dayrider ticket and travelled to the end of the line at Malin Bridge, then rode it back and carried on all the way to the opposite terminus at Halfway. I stared out of the window, longing for Ali and for the palm trees of Luxor.

I thought of his words, *You let me know when you come,* ya *Jen*, and how they were filled with more fear than hope. What was I doing to him, saying I didn't know when I could go back? It wasn't that difficult, was it? All I had to do was access Aunt Carrie's fund and buy a ticket. There was a STA Travel in the Union building – I could get a cheap deal there. Stuff whatever Dad might say. Or Mum, for that matter. I'd take public transport to Gatwick if I had to.

So that's what I did. I went to the bank in the morning and sorted it all out, then I went to STA Travel and got a cheap charter flight to Luxor. It left from Gatwick in mid-December, two days after the end of term, and was a fixed deal for fourteen nights. But somehow I didn't think I'd be using the return flight. I didn't know when I'd come back. I guess I thought I'd stay for the whole of the Christmas holiday at least, but a big part of me wanted to chuck everything in and stay out there for good.

As soon as I'd done it, I felt a load better. I even began to feel more cheerful about student life. The madness of Freshers' Week was finally over and lectures were about to start, so I decided it was time I did some reading. I got a stack of books together and lugged them up to my room. I should say *our* room, because I walked into a beer-and-fags fug and Shell sitting on her desk with her legs wrapped around a hulking rugger bugger. It was eleven a.m., but they were already on the lager. I slammed my books down on my own desk.

'I'm going to do some work,' I informed them. 'And I could do without the company, thanks all the same.'

Shell wriggled on the table and pulled a face. 'Ooooh,' she said. 'Getting stroppy, are we?'

I glared at her. 'You could say that.'

'Gordon Bennett,' said Shell. 'I hope this doesn't mean you're going to be a bore all term.'

I felt myself go scarlet. The last thing that anyone had ever, *ever* been able to accuse me of, up to this point, was being a bore. 'Personally, I find snogging Neanderthals a bit of a bore,' I snapped. 'Are you going to get rid of him or do I have to get someone large enough to do it for you?'

Shell looked a bit taken aback. The Neanderthal didn't have much to say for himself either. He just looked kind of sheepish and extricated himself from between Shell's legs.

'I'd better head off, Shell,' he mumbled and kind of shuffled towards the door.

Shell watched him go, her expression disdainful. Then, once he'd gone, she jumped down from the desk and disappeared into her room. And within twenty minutes, I was reading *The Art of Poetry* to the sound of her gentle snores.

\* \* \*

I thought things might have improved after that. I phoned Ali and told him about the ticket. He sounded pleased and excited, and we worked out that there were twelve weeks to wait before we saw each other again. When you thought about it in weeks, it didn't seem so bad, and I began ticking off the days.

But once the initial elation had subsided, misery returned and got me by the throat. The frenzy of Freshers' Week soon wore off and people settled into groups. The fact was, I hadn't made much of an effort and I didn't *belong* to a group. I'd expended a lot of energy feeling pissed off with Shell, and another load on missing Ali. Sure, I'd *met* lots of people, but there weren't many that I wanted to spend much time with. I would have felt even worse if it hadn't been for Karen, who e-mailed and texted me all the time like the fantastic mate she is. I sometimes heard from Mar, Izzy and a few other old mates from school too, but they all seemed to be thoroughly enjoying themselves in their first term. I was too proud to admit that I wasn't – except to Karen, of course. I think she was a bit worried about me, but I could tell that she was having a brilliant time too, so I tried to play down how I was feeling. There was no point in making her life a misery as well.

Instead, I turned to my work. Unfortunately, poetry isn't really my bag, and that was all we were doing for our core course in the first few weeks. I dreamed my way through the lectures and doodled pictures of feluccas and graceful *galabiyyas* on my notebooks when I was supposed to be working. I bought myself a *Teach Yourself Arabic* book and CD and sat learning that in my spare time.

It wasn't that I wanted to be anti-social. In fact, I hated it – I've never been a loner in my life. But for once, I just couldn't seem to find anyone on my wavelength. It was like everyone else had a different focus and there was no one who understood what I was going through. There were a couple of girls on my corridor who had boyfriends back home, but they just scooted off to visit them at the weekend, or the boyfriends came to Sheffield to see them. When I tried telling them I was seeing someone in Egypt, they looked at me like I was on another planet.

So I grew wary of telling people about Ali. When people asked me if I had a boyfriend, I said I had one back home. It was easier that way. After the first few negative reactions, I didn't want any more. Especially not ones like Shell's.

She'd just launched herself at me, one day. I'd been reading at my desk and for once, so was she. Suddenly, she stood up, wandered around for a minute, then looked down at me.

'I know it's none of my business or anything,' she said confidently, 'but it would do you good to lighten up. You know, like, have some fun.'

I looked up from my books. 'What?'

'F-U-N. Fun,' she said. She had this dark fringe that nearly covered her eyes, and she kind of peered at me from under it. 'I can provide you with a dictionary if you like.'

I felt my hackles rising. Boy, Shell knew how to get to me. 'You're right,' I said shortly. 'It *is* none of your business.'

Shell folded her arms. 'Well, I've got to live with you for a year,' she said. 'Let's face it, we haven't exactly got off to a good start, have we?'

'No,' I agreed. 'We haven't.'

'So maybe we should start, like, talking to each other. I know you talk to *someone* on the payphone. I've seen you. Maybe you could start by telling me who it is?'

I hesitated, thinking. She was right. We had got to put up with each other until at least the end of term. If this was some kind of an olive branch, I should maybe have a go at accepting it. 'My boyfriend,' I said reluctantly.

*Boyfriend.* Of course, that's what he was, but it sounded weird. Boyfriends were what I'd had at school. Boyfriends were guys who got pissed and tried to impress you with their DVD collection, or guys who came to see their girlfriends at the weekend. Somehow Ali didn't fit the description.

'Back home, is he?' asked Shell.

I shook my head. 'No.'

'Ohhhh . . . so he's . . . somewhere else?' Shell raised one eyebrow expressively.

'Yep.'

'Here? That was quick work.' She grinned.

*You can talk*, I thought. 'No. Not here.'

Shell sighed. 'Is this, like, Twenty Questions or something?' she asked. 'Because you might as well come right out with it. From the look of the picture by your bed I'd say he's in Morocco or somewhere.'

I flushed angrily. 'So you've been going through my stuff!'

'Steady,' said Shell. 'I don't think a peek at the little framed number by your bed counts as going through your stuff.'

I just about managed to keep my cool. 'Actually, he's in Egypt,' I said.

Shell snorted. 'Camel-driver, is he?'

I stared at her. 'Are you trying to wind me up? Because if so, you can piss off.'

Shell flopped down in our one-and-only armchair, which was way too small for her. She flung a leg over one arm. 'No,' she said. 'As a matter of fact, I'm not. Honestly. I'm just curious. From where I'm sitting, you're having a crap time when you could be having the time of your life. Don't say you're not, because you are.'

'You're not exactly helping,' I said bitterly.

'Hey, don't try to blame me!' said Shell. 'You're having an awful time because you think you're in love with some bloke thousands of miles away and you don't think anybody cares.'

It was closer to the truth than I was in the mood to admit. I said nothing.

'It just seems a shame to me,' said Shell. Her voice was kind of conciliatory and I guessed she was making an effort, in her own way. 'This place is fantastic. Everyone's having a ball. And you're just sitting around moping, waiting for the end of term.'

I remained silent. I could feel that tears weren't far off and I didn't trust myself to speak.

'I just can't believe he's worth it,' Shell carried on. 'Nobody is – cripes, we're only eighteen. There's plenty of time for serious stuff later. Uni's a once-in-a-lifetime opportunity to let your hair down and you'll really regret it if you don't.' She paused, and studied her nails. 'Well, I would.'

I played with the touchpad on my laptop and didn't look at her. There was a long silence. Shell had obviously finished saying her bit, because she eventually got up and fetched her coat from her bedroom.

'I'm heading down to the Endcliffe for a drink,' she said and I looked up briefly. She gave me a lopsided grin, and I could see she meant well. 'Coming?'

I hesitated. I knew I should take her up on the offer, but I was feeling way too wobbly. I shook my head. Shell shrugged and headed out of the door.

I didn't sleep that night. I lay on my narrow uncomfortable bed staring up at the ceiling, trying to fight back the tears. The last thing I wanted was for Shell to hear me crying. In the end I couldn't stop myself and the tears trickled silently down the sides of my face.

I felt so alone. I knew that everything Shell had said was true. A few months ago, I would have said exactly the same to anyone in my position. Uni was all about having a new start – a whole new adventure. That's what I'd always thought. I'd been looking forward to meeting lots of sexy guys and, as Shell had put it, having a ball. And here I was, only half alive and torn in two.

Maybe I should just let go and have a good time anyway. Ali would want me to be happy. He'd hate to think I was so miserable. Or would he? He was miserable too, waiting for me in Luxor – at least, he sounded it when I spoke to him on the phone. And I guess if I was honest, I'd be a bit upset if he was all chirpy and not missing me at all.

I turned on my side as a voice whispered inside my head. *If you let yourself go, you might start enjoying yourself . . .* That was the worst thing of all. Whatever Shell and everyone else here might think, I knew what I was like. If I went out and did all the stuff I used to do, I'd start flirting with guys. I wouldn't want to and I wouldn't mean to, but they'd come on to me anyway. It would just happen, the way it always had. The thought that I might not be strong enough to resist filled me with shame and misery.

Ali's gorgeous face swam before my mind's eye, his features full of anguish. *I think you make game with me.*

*This just holiday for you, you have nice time with Egyptian man, you go back in England, you forget. This your way, sah?*

'No, Ali,' I whispered to the darkness. 'This not my way. I promised you I'd come back, and I will. I love you and I won't forget you. I'll come back.'

And so the days passed. I felt I was walking a tight-rope – getting on with life just enough to make it bearable, but gazing at my ticket to Luxor every day. We handed in our first essays and I got a C, which was all I could expect given the amount of attention I'd managed to pay to my work. The fact was, I didn't really care.

There was a day looming that I didn't want to face, but I knew I couldn't put it off forever: the day I told Mum and Dad that I was heading straight back to Luxor at the end of term. Since being at Sheffield, I'd had time to think, and that conversation with Mum had stuck in my mind – all that stuff about me being Dad's little girl and him feeling protective of me. She'd said things like that before, but it had never really sunk in. From about the age of twelve, it had just felt like he'd given me grief – didn't want to let me do this, threw a wobbly when I did that. Now that I was abandoning home for Christmas, I felt bad, because I knew it was true that he loved me and worried about me. But what could I do? I was eighteen years old. I'd met a man that I loved and wanted to be with. Dad couldn't change that, whatever he said or did. I just hoped he'd get his head around it, sooner or later.

I was still dreading their response though. Before taking the plunge, I e-mailed Karen, pouring everything out and asking if she could help me in a worst-case scenario. She was brilliant about it and said I could stay with her before leaving if things were too hairy at home. It was good to have a back-up plan, but all the same my hands were sweating when I eventually got round to the Big Deed. It was the last week of term. Of course I should have dealt with it earlier but this way, they wouldn't have much time to react. I soon learned, though, that an awful lot of reaction can be fitted into a very short space of time.

At first, my mum went silent when I told her I'd booked my flight. Then, to my horror, she passed the phone over to Dad. Boy, did he give me what for. Before I knew it, my entire income and education was being thrown into question. He went ballistic and threatened to pull the plug on all my funding. He yelled that I was no daughter of his and that he'd a good mind to disown me altogether. I'd never heard him talk like that and it made me go cold inside. I wanted to say something, anything that would cut through his anger, but I couldn't find any words at all.

It didn't make me change my mind though. I just kept the thought of Ali fixed in my mind's eye, smiling at me. *I'm doing the right thing*, I told myself, over and over, as

Dad raged on. *I am. I'm doing the right thing*. All the same, by the time Mum came back on the phone again I was shaking. I think she was too, because I've never heard her sound like that before – kind of small and alone and distant.

'Dad's just very upset,' she said in this strange, neutral tone.

'He can say what he likes,' I told her, my voice trembling. 'I've got Aunt Carrie's fund. I'm not taking orders from him any more.'

I heard this kind of strangled noise on the other end of the phone. 'We would never jeopardise your education, darling,' said my mum. She could barely get the words out, and that's when I realised she was crying.

# Chapter Eight

I n the end, I did go home. Dad was like this grenade waiting to explode, and I tiptoed around him at first, terrified he'd have another go at me. But he didn't. I could tell he wanted to, but by some miracle of self-control he kept his lips buttoned. And I soon learned that his threats had been pretty empty. He would never fund a trip out to Egypt, of course, but at least he wasn't going to put a stop to everything else or really disown me. In a way, the fact that he had resigned himself to the situation made me feel worse. I guess I might have grown up a bit and I realised that he had been fighting with himself as much as with me, knowing that I had the right to live my own life and that he had to let me go.

As soon as I was on the plane, I shut the UK out. Sheffield, Shell, Dad, Mum, everything. Especially Mum and Dad. It was too painful to think about them. They'd waved me off at the airport and it was awful, knowing I was doing something that they wanted so badly to prevent. I just hoped they'd understand some day, but meanwhile, I had to get on with it. So I just put them into a compartment in the back of my head and slammed the lid.

But as I got closer to Egypt, I got more and more nervous. I'd waited for this all term but the truth was it was pretty scary, flying out there on my own. As the Mediterranean stretched out beneath me, I took lots of deep breaths, telling myself it would all be OK. Ali would be there at the airport with his uncle Tayib. He'd sorted out a flat for me. *For us*, I told myself. My new life – laid out and waiting for me.

And it *was* OK too, when I arrived. The minute I stepped out of the plane, I felt better. Guys in *galabiyyas*, the guttural sounds of Arabic, that smell of dust in the air . . . it was all so familiar, like coming home. The only difference was the temperature – it was much cooler than I'd been expecting. I'd been ready for that blast of heat, but I hadn't twigged; this was December, and Egypt has seasons like anywhere else.

I saw him before he saw me and breathed a sigh of relief. He was wearing jeans and a grey shirt instead of a *galabiyya* and he was smoking, taking quick, nervous drags from his cigarette. From top to toe, he was every bit as gorgeous as I remembered him. He was half-listening to something Tayib was saying and I had a couple of seconds to take in the dark shape of his head, the expressive black eyebrows, the straight back and shoulders. Then he saw me, and I waved.

'Jen!' His face split into a grin and he jogged over. 'You are here. *Il'hamdu lillah!*'

*Thanks be to God.* I knew that now, from learning my bits of Arabic, and I wanted to hug him. I knew we couldn't, because this was Egypt and you couldn't go around hugging people, unless you were two male friends. So I laughed and shook hands instead, first with Ali and then with Tayib.

'It's so good to be back,' I said.

I sat in the front of the taxi, exchanging stolen glances with Ali in the back as we drove through the outskirts of Luxor and out to the bridge over the Nile. The sun was setting, casting a pink glow over the fields and the date palms; workers were on their way home, riding mounds of fodder on their donkeys' backs.

'I find you beautiful flat,' said Ali. 'I think you like it, Jen – this on the west bank, not Luxor side.'

Tayib made a rare comment. 'Near your family,' he said.

*Family.* My heart fluttered, half with pleasure, half with pain, thinking of my own family and the tensions that lay behind me. 'Thank you,' I said, throwing Ali a quick smile. 'I'm sure I'll love it.'

Tayib looked at me appraisingly, nodding, and I felt a bit weird. I still wasn't sure how to read him. I'd never forgotten how he'd responded to us when we first arrived

– how much he'd seemed to resent us, and how Ali had had to persuade him to give us a fair price for taking us to the tombs. There was something about him I didn't trust, and suddenly it seemed odd, him laying claim to me like that. Did he really think of me as a relative? Blimey. Heavy! But there wasn't a lot I could do about it. He was part of the picture, or maybe I was part of his. It was difficult to say.

I pushed the thought aside and soon the taxi was bumping down a dry dirt track and stopping outside a square, blue house. It was one of the modern ones, concrete rather than mud-brick, but without metal struts sticking out of the roof.

'They finish this house,' explained Ali, as he carried my rucksack up to the top floor. 'You have the flat and the roof also.'

The flat had two bedrooms, a spotless kitchen and bathroom and a lounge with a balcony looking out over the fields. It was way more luxurious than Lisa's flat had been. We went up on to the roof and I gasped. It was idyllic. There were colourful mats on the floor, cane furniture dotted around and little lanterns everywhere that Ali quickly lit with his lighter. The house wasn't far from the Pharaoh's stables and I could see a grey Arabian grazing in the twilight under shadowy date palms. I hugged myself in delight, wishing it was Ali I could fling my arms around – but Tayib was still with us.

We went back into the flat and Tayib eventually left.

Alone at last, Ali and I looked at each other uncertainly, our breathing shallow and fast. Then I was in his arms and he was kissing me hungrily. I kissed him in return, letting myself go, letting all the hassle and strain of the last three months drain out of me. His fingers reached inside my top and up my back, stroking my skin and drawing me closer. I pulled his shirt out of his jeans and ran my hand up to his chest, feeling where his muscles were taut from handling the felucca. Then he pulled my hips tight against his and I knew that this was what I wanted so badly, wanted more than I'd ever wanted anything.

And then he stopped. Suddenly. I was taken completely by surprise. I looked at him, and his eyes were wide. He was listening.

'What is it?' I managed to ask.

'I hear something,' said Ali. 'Maybe . . .' He trailed off and pulled away from me, hurriedly stuffing his shirt back into his jeans. He went to the door and placed his ear against it.

'What is it?' I repeated, more insistently this time. I felt like someone had chucked a bucket of cold water over me.

Ali came away from the door, his eyebrows furrowed. 'I think maybe someone come,' he said. He grinned. 'But nobody there. Everything OK, *ya* Jen.'

I was baffled. I stepped towards him and touched his arm, but the moment had gone. Ali seemed ill at ease, even slightly frightened, and I didn't understand.

'Whose is this flat, anyway?' I asked, looking around. I really hadn't expected anything this swanky. 'I'm not sure I can afford it, Ali.'

'This no problem,' said Ali. 'This the flat of uncle of my friend. They make for tourists but I get you good price because you stay long time. Same price Lisa's flat. This OK with you?'

I stared. 'Are you sure?'

'Sure, sure.'

'Well, in that case . . .' I opened my arms out wide. 'It's fantastic!'

Ali looked relieved, and pleased. He lit a Cleopatra and seemed to relax again. 'You want take shower?' he asked. 'You hungry? I go and bring something for eat.'

'OK. That would be great. I'll give you some money . . .'

I picked up my moneybelt from the table, but Ali stopped me. 'Jen,' he said softly, turning me round to face him. 'I don't want that you worry, OK? I buy you dinner and we have nice time, relax. You in Egypt now. With me.'

I nearly said, *Look who's talking*. It wasn't me who'd leapt to the door just when we were getting somewhere. But I didn't. I put my arms around his waist and gave him a soft kiss on the lips. 'OK,' I said. 'I'll give you your presents when you get back.'

'Presents?' Ali's eyes widened.

'Don't get too excited,' I said, giving him a squeeze.

'Anyway you're not getting anything until you've bought me my dinner.'

He laughed. 'I come back soon,' he said. 'I lock the door, OK?' He picked up the keys to the flat and put them in his pocket. It was only when he'd gone that I realised there was only one set.

Once I was on my own in the flat, I felt suddenly scared. It was quiet here – much quieter than in central Luxor. There were neighbouring houses and I heard the bray of a donkey, but I didn't have a clue where I was. I was just in a strange house in the middle of nowhere. It all made me feel a bit panicky. I checked the lock – it was some kind of mortis, so I couldn't leave until Ali came back with the keys. What was worse, something had freaked him out and I had no idea what.

To calm my nerves, I unpacked my rucksack and tried out the shower as Ali had suggested. I soon found out that it looked better than it worked, but it wasn't too bad and I stood under the sputtering water, thinking. I knew about the tourist police, the special branch that was supposed to look after the interests of foreigners and keep tourist sites safe. The locals hated them because they were so heavy-handed – people in the company of Westerners were always being stopped and questioned. But I didn't see how they could know I was here, or how it could be a problem. Was it the flat owners that Ali was worried about, I wondered? Had he really got me such a good price? Did he think that someone might barge in on us? Maybe the owners had keys too.

That thought got me out of the shower pretty quickly. I dressed nervously, then wandered out on to the balcony to wait. A wind had risen, blowing the date palms, and a dog started howling mournfully nearby. It gave me the heebie-jeebies and I shivered. Then, to my relief, I soon saw Ali walking back towards the house along the track. I waved and he lifted a plastic bag in greeting.

'I'm so glad you're back,' I gasped, once he'd let himself back in. 'It felt strange here on my own.'

'This not good flat?' he asked, looking anxious.

'Oh! Yes. The flat's great. It's just that you thought someone was coming, before, and I don't have any keys . . .'

Ali raised his hand. 'No worry, Jen,' he said reassuringly. 'Everything OK. The keys for you. Look, we eat.'

He had bought spit-roasted chicken quarters, vegetable stew and rice, and we found plates and cutlery in the kitchen. With Ali bustling around with me, everything felt normal again. It was fun, having our own place. We moved the table close to the balcony and ate looking out over the fields. We could see the twinkling lights of a village somewhere out there and though we were some distance from the river, we could still hear the rhythmic croaking of frogs in the reeds.

When we'd finished, we cleared the plates away and I fetched his presents from my bag. The first was a compilation tape of my favourite music – I'd made it in my room at home before going to uni. The second was a bit extravagant but I didn't care. I handed him a box wrapped in silver paper.

Ali looked like a little kid. He unwrapped it slowly, like he was scared of tearing the paper.

'What this, *ya* Jen?' he asked in amazement, as he opened the box.

'It's a sports watch,' I told him. 'It's waterproof. In case you get it wet in the felucca.' I looked at him, suddenly worried. 'Don't you like it?'

'Jen!' He shook his head, a weird mixture of pleasure and disbelief on his face. 'Yes, yes. Of course. I like it too much.'

He grinned and reached to kiss me. Then stopped. This time I heard it too – the sound of footsteps coming up the stairs. Looking suddenly terrified, Ali shoved the watch and the box into my lap. 'Hide this,' he whispered. Then, before I could say anything, he slipped silently across the room and up the steps that led to the roof.

Someone hammered on the door. My heart pounding, I shoved the watch under the sofa cushion and picked up the keys from the table.

'Who's there?' I called.

'This the tourist police,' replied a male voice. 'You must open.'

*Tourist police!* My hands were shaking as I fumbled with the keys. Eventually I managed to open the door to find two guys in uniform standing there.

'Hello,' I said. My voice came out in a squeak.

'You stay here?' they asked me.

I nodded.

'We come in, please. You show us your passport.'

I backed into the room, reached for my moneybelt and handed over my passport. I couldn't believe this was happening.

'And Ali Ibrahim? He is here?'

I gaped at them. 'Ali?'

'Yes, Ali.' The guy had a nasty look in his eye. 'Ali Ibrahim.'

I had no idea what Ali could have done wrong, but I had the sense to keep my mouth shut. 'N-no,' I stuttered. 'No. He's not here.'

'But he stay here? With you?'

I shook my head, trying not to look at the sofa. I was terrified there might be some wrapping paper sticking out from under the cushion. 'No. He found me the flat but he's not staying here.'

The guys stared at me for a moment, then one walked into the kitchen and the other climbed the stairs to the roof. My heart was in my mouth and I didn't know what to do. The only thing I could think of was to walk over to the sofa and sit down – at least that way, they wouldn't find the watch.

I wiped my hands on my jeans. They were wet with sweat. The second guy walked out of the kitchen and looked in the bedrooms. I prayed that the guy wouldn't find Ali on the roof, though I couldn't see how he wouldn't. But then, to my relief, I saw him coming back down again. He called his mate and they had a fast conversation in Arabic.

Then they turned to me. 'Sorry we disturb you,' said one of them. He didn't sound particularly sorry though. He leered and added, 'Have a nice stay.'

They walked out of the door and closed it behind them. I got up and locked it. Then I burst into tears.

I slumped on to the sofa. I don't know how long I sat there. I stopped crying and stared through the window into the night, feeling lost and shaken. Then, when I heard footsteps on the stairs again, I jumped.

'*Ya* Jen,' called a quiet voice through the door. 'This Ali. You let me in?'

The relief felt like a cool shower and I rushed to the door.

'What happened to you? Where did you go? Did they see you?' I gabbled, as soon as he stepped inside.

'I go down the side.' He showed me his hands, which looked grazed and filthy. I guessed he had managed to scramble down a drainpipe or something.

'Oh, God, Ali. Here, come and wash them. Do they hurt?'

He shook his head. 'Not much.' He followed me obediently into the bathroom and began to wash his hands. 'You OK?' he asked me.

I nodded. 'They checked my passport and searched the flat. I was terrified they'd find you on the roof.' I stared at him. 'Ali, what did they want? Why were they looking for you?'

Ali wiped his hands on a towel. 'This Mohammed al-Saeed,' he said. 'I know this.' He pursed his lips angrily. 'Man in Gurna village. I make argument with him last week. So he say to tourist police and they come.'

I was baffled. 'What are you talking about?'

Ali sighed. 'Mohammed angry because I give him money long time ago and then I ask him for it back. He say to me, how you need money? You have nice English friend, you not need the money. We make big argument, like this way. He is . . .' Ali searched for the word.

I frowned. 'Jealous?' I hazarded.

'Yes.' Ali nodded. 'And so you see, he make problem for me.'

'But . . . I don't get it,' I protested. Ali was talking as though everything was perfectly obvious, but I still couldn't work it out. 'What have the tourist police got to do with it? What have you done wrong?'

There was a rustle outside and we both looked at the door, tense. Seconds ticked by and nothing happened. Ali walked to the door and listened intently, then turned to me. 'Jen, I need go. If they come and I here, they put me in the prison. Maybe you also.' He took my hands in his and I could sense his unhappiness. 'This Egypt, *ya* Jen. Not England.' He sighed heavily. 'I think tomorrow you stay in hotel. Better this way, *sah?*'

I nodded. I was dumbfounded. Nothing made any sense, but after the events of the day the thought of a nice, safe hotel was pretty appealing. 'OK,' I said.

'I sorry . . .' Ali's eyes searched mine. 'You OK here tonight, by yourself? I not think they come again. Maybe they look for me with my family.'

I could see I didn't have much choice, so I nodded. Ali looked so sorrowful. I hugged him; we stood in silence, holding each other. Then he pulled away.

'I bring Tayib in the morning,' he said. 'You find nice hotel.'

I spent the next day checking out what was on offer on the west bank, but I ended up back on the 'Luxor side', as Ali called it. Knowing that the tourist police had their eye on me, I wanted to feel more anonymous and the bustle of the town itself definitely helped.

Things still felt pretty weird. I hadn't expected to feel culture shocked, but I did. And what I wanted to do more than anything was tell someone about it. There was no Lisa, not this time; I knew she'd returned to Germany some time in September. So while Ali dealt with some business with his father, I hunted out an

Internet café near the *souq* and sat down to write to Karen.

I'd just finished pouring everything out – I don't think I've ever typed so fast in my life – when I noticed the woman at the next computer. She was watching me curiously, and looked kind of familiar.

'Aren't you a friend of Lisa's?' she said to me.

I did a double take. 'Yeah,' I said. I still couldn't quite place her though. 'You know her too?'

'Yes, I was here in the summer,' she said. 'I met you in Lisa's flat. I'm Tina.'

'I'm Jen,' I told her.

*Tina*. It rang bells, and I did remember meeting her now. She was English and I guess she was in her fifties. I smiled and turned to pay the Internet guy who was hovering over my shoulder.

'Do you want to go for a *shai*?' asked Tina. 'I'm just finishing too.'

I hesitated, but not for long. Ali wouldn't be free for a couple of hours and I reckoned that any new friends and allies had to be a good thing, even though I knew I'd never spend time with someone like Tina at home. She looked older than my Mum!

We went and sat in one of the tourist cafés near Luxor Temple. We ordered two glasses of *shai* and I explained I'd just got back.

'Are you seeing someone here?' she asked me, straight out.

I blushed. 'Is it that obvious?' I responded.

Tina grinned. 'Well, you're not an Egyptologist, and that's the other main reason why people come back to Luxor.'

'So are *you* an Egyptologist?' I asked her quickly.

She laughed. 'No. I'm just different. I've been coming here a long time. Seen it all, done it all, got the T-shirt. Despite everything I still love it all and I come back whenever I can, just to relax. I'm here for a month this time – it's my Christmas treat.' She gave me a friendly, knowing smile. 'You're not exactly the usual type yourself, you know.'

'The usual type?'

'The type that comes back.'

I frowned, not sure what she meant.

'You're young and attractive with a life to live,' she carried on. 'Sure, there are plenty of girls your age who have a holiday fling here, but most of them go home and forget about it. The women who get involved out here are usually older. Much older. My age. It's the same old story – rich, older women. Young, tasty men.'

My stomach churned. *Not this again*, I thought. I was sick of hearing about how everyone exploited everyone else in Luxor. 'Yeah, well, I guess I am different,' I agreed, a bit abruptly. 'So's Ali.'

'Ali.' Tina smiled. 'So that's his name. Where are you staying?'

I thought of the tourist police banging on the door of the flat. I hesitated. I could just give the name of the hotel but suddenly I knew I wanted to understand, and I had the feeling that Tina could explain. I decided to tell her the truth. 'I was going to stay in a flat on the west bank but the tourist police came, so I've moved back over here, to a hotel.'

Tina's eyebrows shot up. 'The police actually came?'

'Yes. They were looking for Ali. I still don't know why to be honest.'

'He didn't tell you?'

I felt uncomfortable. My heart started beating faster, but Tina's voice was gentle and I got the feeling I could trust her. 'No,' I admitted. 'He said something about some guy being jealous. It didn't make sense.'

Tina was now all attention, sitting on the edge of her seat. She looked at me intently. 'Well, you did the right thing to move,' she said. 'You know, I've heard of lots of things here in Luxor, but I've never met anyone who's actually had the police search their flat. It's talked about all the time, though. Everyone knows it can happen.'

'But why?' I asked.

Tina looked surprised. 'You really don't know . . . ?' she trailed off, shaking her head. Then she suddenly laid her hand over mine on the table. 'This isn't England, you know. It's Egypt. It's a military state run on Islamic lines. You have to do things differently. You can be arrested for spending the night with someone – unless you're married, of course.'

My mouth dropped open. '*Arrested?*'

'Yes. Arrested. Though it would be much worse for Ali than it would for you. And what's more, it's a close-knit community and everyone loves to gossip. It's pretty much impossible to rent a flat on the west bank without people seeing what's going on. And not everyone's going to take kindly to it, for any number of reasons. The whole place festers with rivalries.'

I let out my breath slowly.

'This is an old, old community, Jen,' Tina carried on. 'Especially on the west bank. Times are slowly changing but you'd be astonished how much remains the same. The *fellaheen*, the peasants, have been tilling the fields here since Pharaonic times. Of course most people are Muslim now but you'll still get women creeping into the ancient temples at night to beg for fertility . . .'

She drifted off for a moment, seemingly lost in thought. 'So you see,' she said, 'a young, apparently affluent Westerner like you comes along and stirs up pretty deep waters. All it takes is someone to get jealous and – well, there you have it. The tourist police are at your door.'

I gaped at her. Of course I wasn't really surprised by what she was telling me – I'd seen enough of things over the summer to have some idea of how things worked. I knew there was so much I didn't know and might never understand. But the truth is, I didn't think anything would happen to *me*.

'But why didn't Ali tell me?' I said, thinking aloud. 'Why risk getting the flat?'

Tina shrugged and gave me a wry smile. 'I don't know your Ali,' she said. 'But my guess is that he's a very proud man in more ways than one. They all are. He wanted you over there in a flat and he didn't want to admit to his fears about it. He was probably hoping you'd get away with it. A lot of people do, though most don't risk it for long. You were unlucky to be investigated so quickly but like I said, you stand out. You're a young girl and it wouldn't be difficult to get the tourist police to take an interest. They have to make sure that nothing happens to you because if it did, the Egyptian tourist industry would pay the price. Imagine the headlines back home.'

I couldn't, or maybe I didn't want to. But I knew exactly what she meant about standing out. I was silent.

'Hasn't Ali talked to you about getting married?' asked Tina, after a pause.

'*Married*?' I knew I was coming across as really, really naïve but I was too gob-smacked to care.

'It's the only way forward,' said Tina gently. 'If you're serious about this guy, that is, and you're sure he's honest. If you're not, you're better off not getting involved.'

My mouth was dry. I wanted to push the table away and shout at her. Dammit, she was a just a stranger, a woman who'd accosted me in an Internet café. *What do you know?* I wanted to shout. *Who are you? Why do you have to interfere?*

But on another level I knew that she was telling me the truth and that I had to listen. 'Yes, I'm serious about him,' I muttered.

Tina studied her fingers. 'There's a thing called an *orfi* marriage,' she said. 'It's an unregistered marriage – just a bit of paper. If you get one, you're free to do as you please. You can have your relationship and no one will bother you. You just produce your bit of paper when questioned and you tear it up when you leave.'

*Marriage. Paper. Questioning.* It was all too much to take in. 'I can't do that,' I protested. I felt panicked. 'I don't know enough about everything here.'

'Well, perhaps you won't need to yet, as you're back in a hotel,' said Tina. 'But you have to be very, very careful. If he's worth it and if you want to make life easier, it's the only way, I'm afraid – for your own protection and for Ali's.'

Her voice had come over all maternal and I felt like screaming again. 'I think I can look after myself,' I said. I decided to change the subject. 'So how do you know Lisa?'

Tina looked at me for a long moment before answering. Half of me wanted to know what she was thinking. The other half didn't. Anyway, I could guess: she thought I was out of my depth. Maybe I was.

'I knew Lisa's mother,' she said eventually.

'Oh, back in Germany?'

'No,' said Tina. 'Here. Lisa never told you?'

I shook my head, bracing myself. Something suddenly told me that I was in for another nasty revelation and I wasn't sure how many more I could handle.

'Lisa's mother Greta used to bring Lisa here in her holidays. She first came when Lisa was thirteen, fourteen, something like that. She was a divorcee and she fell for a Luxor guy called Gamal. When Lisa went to university they got married and she sold up everything she had in Germany to build a house here.'

Tina paused. I got the feeling she'd told this story many times before. 'Gamal wanted to set up a tourist restaurant as well as build the house. Because she didn't speak or write Arabic, she had to trust him with all the negotiations. There were endless builders' fees, deposit fees for the restaurant, legal fees – you name it. And she provided money until she'd been sucked dry. In the end, the restaurant never materialised. I think there was a piece of land, but the house was never finished. It turned out that most of the money had gone to Gamal's first wife and seven children out in a village somewhere.'

A caleche clip-clopped by on the street and the driver waved at us with a brown tobacco-stained smile. I looked away. 'So what happened in the end?' I asked.

'Greta never recovered. She'd lost everything. She went

back to Germany and had a breakdown.' Tina sighed. 'I heard that she died last year.'

There was a tight, constricting feeling in my chest. I swallowed. 'So why does Lisa come back?' I managed to ask.

Tina shrugged. 'I don't really know,' she said. 'Maybe she needs to find a reason. Wouldn't you?'

# Chapter Nine

I was still thinking about it when I met Ali later that day. I wondered why Lisa had never told me her story when she warned me about the men here, and then I realised I probably wouldn't have wanted to hear it back in the summer. Now it seemed like everything was clearer and a little bit colder, as though the change in season had given me a change in understanding too. Life here was hard. I knew that. People were poor. Some of them would do almost anything to make money and Western women were an easy target.

But I didn't have any money, or not much; and anyway, Ali was different. I was sure of that. I walked along the Corniche and looked down over the parapet to where the *Ali Baba* was moored. Ali had a dustpan and brush and was sweeping out the inside of the boat, a Cleopatra dangling from his mouth. He was back in his usual pale blue *galabiyya*, and I watched him for a moment as a deep, aching love swelled inside me. Whatever this incredible community was all about, I was sure we could find a way through it.

I ran lightly down the path to the feluccas and called. Ali looked up, his face lighting up as he saw me. I clambered on to the *Ali Baba* and flopped on to the cushions.

'The hotel is OK?' Ali asked me. He shook his head sorrowfully. 'I am very sorry about this . . . the flat. This crazy government . . . Not this way in England, *sah?*'

'*Sah*,' I agreed. 'It's pretty different. But the hotel's fine. Don't worry, Ali.'

Ali put the brush and pan away under the deck and sat down next to me. The felucca rocked gently and I rested my head on his shoulder briefly, turning my face to the sun. It was a beautiful warm, golden sun now, not the sweltering orb of summer.

'How I not worry?' he asked softly. 'This not what we want.'

I looked at him. 'I met someone this morning. An English woman,' I told him. 'She told me that I have to marry you. She said it's the only way we'll both be safe.'

Ali looked at his hands and said nothing.

'Is it true?' I asked.

His shoulders sagged, and he nodded. 'Yes. But I know this not England way, and I make frighten – I think if I say this, maybe you not come back . . .'

'Oh, Ali.' I squeezed his arm. 'You should have trusted me.'

His face suddenly filled with hope. 'You mean . . . maybe you like to be my wife? This not problem for you?'

I did a double take. That wasn't what I'd meant. 'Oh – well . . . I'm not sure,' I stuttered.

Ali's face contracted in disappointment. He reached for his packet of Cleopatras. I frowned, thinking. There was something that I'd never voiced before and I wondered how Ali would react.

'I don't know,' I said. 'I was thinking that maybe you'd like to come to England.'

Ali laughed. '*Ya salaam!*' he exclaimed. 'Ah, *ya* Jen, if I come in England, how I work the felucca?'

'Well . . . you could find other work.'

'But my mother, my sisters, they need eat.' Ali hesitated. '*Ya* Jen, I am only man in my family. My father make sick, not strong for the felucca now. The medicine for him very expensive. I pay this now, but how I pay if I go in England?'

'But doesn't the government pay for his medicine?' I asked.

'*Yani* . . . the government pay some thing. But not the good medicine for my father. I need I pay this.'

I was shocked, but at the same time I was impressed with Ali. He loved his family so much and I felt a pang of something – envy, jealousy, something like that. I wasn't sure. I had spent so long trying to kick free from my own family and, at that moment, I felt kind of sad that I'd succeeded.

I thought for a minute. 'But if you worked in England, you might earn more,' I said. 'You could send them the money.'

Ali shook his head dismissively. 'Forget it. This crazy talk, *ya* Jen. I never make passport.'

'You don't have a passport?' Even as the words came out of my mouth, though, I realised it was a dumb question. Of course he didn't have a passport. It was one of the things that poorer Egyptian men were all supposed to be after, via Westerners. It was weird, realising how I'd always taken my own passport totally for granted and just how privileged I was.

Ali shook his head. 'This very expensive,' he said. 'Also visa for England big problem. Maybe this possible after marry, but *orfi* marriage no good for this. We have to go to Cairo and make marriage in big *maktab* . . .'

He looked at me questioningly. 'Office?' I guessed.

Ali nodded, and carried on. 'But I think they still don't let me come. This not easy, *ya* Jen. They want to know how I make money in England, and what I say? Felucca. You have felucca in England?'

I shook my head.

'So you see,' said Ali. 'This not possible. Felucca is all I know. I not finish exam in the school. I know about this because my cousin meet English woman and try to go in England. The *maktab* in Cairo never make him these papers. He stay and she go.'

I was silent. I watched as a black and white kingfisher hovered above the water, further out over the Nile. It dived, making a little splash. I looked further, over to the mountains on the west bank, now lost in the shimmer of the late afternoon heat. Despite the hardships of living here, it was difficult to see why anyone would want to exchange it for soggy, grey England. I sighed. There was nothing for it. I was going to have to think about staying here.

As it had done in the summer, the time began to slip by. We lounged in the felucca, munching on *termis* beans and spitting their yellow skins into the water. We rode through the sugarcane fields on horseback. We played pool on a decrepit table in a dusty old hotel on the west bank, where it looked as though there hadn't been any tourists for a decade. We bought cheap beer from secret dealers in the middle of nowhere and drank it at local wedding parties. It was nearly Christmas but the sun was shining and I didn't give a damn.

Well, almost. I guess we both needed some time, because we just settled back into our old routine with me staying in the hotel. We avoided talk of passports or marriage or the tourist police. All the same, things were different now. I was aware of Ali's nervousness when we were out together. I realised that staying in a flat together wasn't the only issue; he could be questioned at any time because of me. I remembered the first time I'd taken him for dinner – how I'd thought he was nervous because of the other tourists. Now I knew better. He wasn't safe, and he wouldn't be safe until I married him.

And so I was thinking. All the time. Thinking about how I could find a way of making it work. After a few days, we talked, walking back from a wedding in a village out beyond Medinet Habu. It was cold at night now, and once we were in the safety of the sugarcane fields Ali put his arm around me and we walked with our hips moving in time.

'I wish you could come back to the hotel with me,' I told him. 'It's so difficult, having to hide. And I worry about the tourist police.'

Ali said nothing, but pulled me a little closer.

'I wish we could just get married,' I said. 'But I'm afraid. I'm not ready yet. There's so much I don't understand . . .'

'No worry, *ya* Jen,' Ali interrupted me. 'Are you happy? This the important thing.'

'Yes. Yes, I'm happy. But . . .'

'Then I wait for you.'

I looked up at his face. His expression was full of tenderness, so much tenderness I thought my heart would burst. We stopped walking and kissed.

'This my way,' whispered Ali, running his lips over my forehead and round to my ear. 'I not like the men on the

Corniche. Maybe you not think this but I am good Muslim man. I wait. You see, *ya* Jen. I wait.'

I felt moved. I felt tears gather in my throat and I swallowed them back down. 'Thank you, Ali,' I murmured.

'No. I thank you,' he responded quietly. 'I am so happy that you come back. So, so happy. And one day I hope you my wife, but not yet. When you ready. I love you, Jen. I wait.'

I lifted my hand to his cheek and traced the line of his eyebrow with my finger. 'I love you too, Ali,' I said. I smiled. 'We'll wait together.'

But I still had to work out what to do. It was easy to know what *not* to do: I hated Sheffield so much that I didn't care about going back. My education could wait, and anyway it wouldn't be much use out here as far as I could see. Money was a bigger issue though. My fund wasn't going to last long – a few months, tops. And I couldn't rely on Ali. He was already supporting his whole family and I wasn't going to let him support me. I churned everything around in my mind, determined to find a way forward.

I saw Tina every couple of days. It was good to know there was someone who knew the score, and I'd meet her for a glass of hibiscus tea, called *kerkedi*, in a *sheesha* café in Luxor.

'How do women survive here?' I asked her one day. 'I mean the Western ones. Do any of them work?'

Tina grinned. 'They bring their money with them, of course,' she said. 'That's the point.'

'I know that,' I persisted. 'But there must be *some* people who work, surely?'

'A few businesses are owned by foreigners,' said Tina, with a shrug. 'But most people who work here are based in Cairo. Unless they've come to do something specific, like Egyptology. Why?'

I blew on the hot, sweet hibiscus tea. 'I'll need to find something if I stay.'

Tina looked at me strangely. 'You *have* got it bad, haven't you?' she commented.

I flushed. 'You think I'm crazy, don't you?' I muttered.

Tina smiled. 'No,' she said. 'I don't. You haven't done anything daft, as far as I can see. You're not handing over lots of money, are you?'

I shook my head.

'Good,' said Tina. 'And neither should you. A felucca captain can earn in a week what a hospital doctor earns in a month.'

'You're kidding!' I gasped.

'Oh yes,' said Tina. She gave a wry smile. 'Mind you, that's not saying much. Doctors' wages are shocking.' She shrugged. 'It's all just a question of scale. Anyway, the point is that you're looking after yourself. And who knows? Everyone can tell you till they're blue in the face what to do or what will happen, but every person on this planet is different. The only way to find out whether something can work is to try it out for yourself.'

I felt a warm rush of gratitude. 'Thanks, Tina,' I said. 'I wish my family saw it like that. I've really stuck my neck out, coming back.'

'They're bound to worry,' she replied. 'If you were my daughter, I would.' She paused. 'So you're not getting an *orfi*, then?'

I shook my head. 'Not yet. I told Ali I wasn't ready and I'm staying in the hotel.'

Tina raised an eyebrow. 'Good for you,' she said. 'And what did he say?'

'That he was happy to wait.'

'An honourable Muslim. Even better,' said Tina, with a grin. 'You know, you might have got yourself a good man there.'

'I think so,' I said, laughing. 'But I'm biased.'

Tina took a final swig of *kerkedi*, swirling the syrupy red liquid around her glass. 'Well,' she said. 'I know a few people here. I'll ask around, see if anyone knows of a bit of work you could do. Whatever it is, it won't pay very well and you won't be able to live like a Westerner indefinitely. You'd have to move out of the hotel, which will obviously raise all the other questions.'

I nodded. 'I know. But I've got enough money for now,' I said. I didn't really want to think about how it would be when it ran out.

\* \* \*

The next day it was Christmas. It was totally weird, waking up in my hotel room with the sun blazing outside and the sound of the muezzins calling from the mosques, just like any other Thursday morning. I didn't think I'd care, but I switched on my mobile and found a stack of texts all wishing me Happy Christmas. They kind of caught me sideways and my eyes blurred with tears.

I sent a few texts back, then made my way slowly down to the river and across on the ferry to find Ali. We usually ate breakfast in a little *fuul* and *taamiya* joint, and sure enough he was waiting for me there, reading an Arabic newspaper.

'What's happening in the world then?' I asked in a doleful tone as I sat down heavily on the bench opposite. To be honest, I was feeling pretty wobbly. I knew very well what was happening in *my* world. It was cold and there were lights everywhere and Christmas trees and people opening presents. Mum would already be fretting about the turkey and everyone would soon be drinking too much and squabbling about whether to watch *The Great Escape* or *Top of the Pops*.

Ali closed the paper and looked at me. 'Christmas is happening,' he said. A slow smile spread over his features. 'You think I not know this? Happy Christmas, *habibi*.'

And from the bench beside him he picked up a little box wrapped in red paper and handed it to me. I was gobsmacked.

'Take it,' he said.

I wanted to hug him, but the guys in the café were watching – in fact they were all laughing at my expression, and made joshing remarks to Ali in Arabic. He looked around at them, grinning, and called something back.

My fingers trembling, I tore off the red paper and found a little jewellery box. Slowly, I lifted the lid. I gasped. Inside was a silver chain, with a beautiful silver *ankh* dangling from it – the ancient Egyptian symbol of life that looked just like the Christian cross but with a loop at the top. I stared at it. I could tell it wasn't a cheap piece of junk from the *souq*. It was gorgeous and I felt overwhelmed with emotion.

'It's beautiful,' I managed to say, desperately trying to hold back the waterworks. I didn't want to cry, not here, and I kept my head bowed.

'This the life,' he told me, pointing to the *ankh*. 'You know this?'

I nodded. 'Yes, I know.' A tear escaped down my cheek.

'Jen. You OK?' Ali's voice was all concern.

I felt I was trying to suppress a geyser and I couldn't answer. I don't really know what got into me. I was all over the place and I knew I had to get out of there before I made a real fool of myself, so I swung my legs off the bench and almost ran down the road. There a little track that led off into the fields so I headed down it blindly until I was away from all the buildings. I sat on a rock and let the tears flow.

'Jen! *Ya* Jen, *ay fee*? What is it?' Ali had caught up with me. He crouched down to peer anxiously into my face, and I saw that he was holding the box and the *ankh* necklace. I reached out for them and he placed them in my hands, but even so I just carried on crying.

I didn't know what to say. It was just everything, and *everything* was too difficult to put into specific words just then. It was the hot sun at Christmas and eating *fuul* for breakfast. It was trying to understand too much at once and trying not to care about the things that didn't fit. It was the terrible story of Lisa's mum and all the other stories like it. It was the way everyone here was poor with so little hope of anything ever changing. And more than anything it was Ali, who I loved so much. It was the necklace that I knew he couldn't afford even if felucca captains *did* make more money than doctors.

Ali stroked my arm while I tried to pull myself together. Soon, I grew calmer, and gave him a watery smile.

'I'm OK – really . . .' I said. 'Sometimes I'm just so confused.'

Ali's eyes were full of understanding. 'I know this,' he said. 'Don't worry. I do anything for you. All I want is that you happy.'

'Do you think everything is going to be OK?' I whispered, searching his face. I knew he didn't have the answers any more than I did, but I wanted to hear him reassure me. The fact was that in Egypt, he was all I had.

I should have guessed that the answer would be as Egyptian as he was himself.

'*Insh'allah,*' he said. '*Insha'allah*, everything will be OK.'

So that was it – Christmas in the desert. Once I was feeling a bit less wobbly, I rang home and spoke to my mum. She said that she'd bought me presents as usual and that we'd have a mini-Christmas in January when I got home. She said that they were having a nice time, but that Toby was already immersed in his new PlayStation game and Dad had fallen asleep in front of the TV. I detected a note of loneliness in her voice and that was when I realised how much she was missing me.

I fingered the *ankh* around my neck, wishing I could show it to her. When she talked about me going home in January, I heard how her voice quickened – how she was almost afraid to mention it in case I said I wasn't going back, but how she couldn't resist saying it anyway. I never would have noticed something like that before. I'd changed, these last few months. I'd started feeling the pain of life's complications. Of course, I thought I'd felt it before, but now I knew that the ups and downs I'd gone through at school were mild compared to what I'd seen since leaving.

The rest of the day was kind of tinged with sweet sadness. I went out in the felucca with Ali and we watched the sunset together. I felt glad that I'd chosen to be here instead of the UK, but I was beginning to understand that there were gaps. Big, friend-and-family-sized gaps, culture gaps and gaps in understanding. We could work at them forever and they'd never be completely filled in. I reflected on how I was here because I was free – because I was a Western woman who could leave her family behind. Ali was different. He was tied to this place, to his people and to the river Nile, and I was beginning to understand that he never imagined leaving. It was a lot to take in, and a lot to accept. But as Ali's eyes met mine in the pink-gold evening light and I fingered the unfamiliar chain around my neck, I felt sure in my heart that he was worth it.

Just as Christmas had done, Boxing Day dawned like any other day – bright and clear and gorgeous. I sat in the Internet café and sent Karen a long e-mail about everything that had been going on and how I was looking for a way to stay here and earn money. I explained that I hadn't seen Tina but I was still hopeful that she'd sort something out. I told her about Christmas and Ali and the *ankh*, and how it had made me cry. I told her I missed her and wished she was out here with me.

I'd started a more lighthearted message to Mar when I got a reply from Karen, asking me if middle-class Egyptians used babysitters. That made me laugh – like anyone had less than about fifteen relatives within shouting distance! It got me thinking though. There must be something that people needed here – not families like Ali's on the west bank, but maybe the middle-class ones in the town. I'd have to ask Tina and see what she said.

When I went down to the Corniche to find Ali, I only found a couple of his tout friends hanging about.

'Tourists come,' they said to me. 'He take the felucca. Banana Island.'

'Oh, OK,' I nodded. I peered up the Nile. I could see a few felucca sails but they were all too far off for me to make out the *Ali Baba*. 'I'll come back later.'

I decided to take a book and pay to lounge by the Horizon pool for a couple of hours. The late December days were perfect for sunbathing, like a hot English summer without any of the mugginess. I looked through the books I'd brought with me – *The Adventures of Huckleberry Finn* and Katherine Mansfield's *Selected Stories*. They were my course books. I'd felt so confused when I was packing that I'd shoved them in, knowing I was supposed to be handing in an essay in January based on them. Now I knew that I wouldn't be doing *that*, so I shoved them to one side and picked out *The Map of Love* by Ahdaf Soueif instead.

The Horizon pool was packed with more tourists than I'd ever seen in the whole time I'd spent there in the summer. That was high season for you – everyone was here getting their bit of winter sun. I had a job finding a lounger and knew that once I'd landed one I'd have to guard it with my life.

Maybe that was why I didn't get up when everyone else did. Not right away. There was some commotion out on the river and I decided to ignore it.

Then I heard an American woman almost shrieking. 'My God, they're going to hit it!'

That made me look up. Who and what was hitting what? The crowd of tourists staring out over the Nile had grown and I had to crane my neck to see what was going on. I could see one of the big cruise ships out in the middle of the river and I heard the blast of its horn. Then I spotted a row of tourists on the top deck, all peering over the barrier in alarm.

What I couldn't see was the sail of the felucca – someone said it had been there – because by then it was already deep underwater, somewhere beneath the cruise ship's hull.

As soon as I heard someone mention the word *felucca*, I didn't hang around. I ran to my lounger, threw my clothes on over my bikini and grabbed my stuff. Sprinting out of the hotel and down the Corniche, I started praying: *Please let it not be Ali. Please.*

I could see that the river police boats were out in force. Down by the ferry, there were throngs in *galabiyyas*, all gossiping and calling to each other at the tops of their voices. I plunged down among them, looking for familiar faces. There had to be someone I knew, someone I recognised. I couldn't see anyone so I resorted to my bits of Arabic, tapping on people's shoulders and asking, *'Meen? Meen?'*

*Who? Who?*

Men turned to look at me, but their eyes were unseeing. Their gaze just drifted over this white European girl and moved away, back to their friends and to the drama unfolding on the river. Desperate, I tried to understand the streams of words all around me, listening for names. I couldn't glean a thing.

And then I heard it. *Ali Baba. Ali Baba.* I had this weird feeling, like there was a slab of ice sliding down my whole body and freezing me to the spot. While men jabbered and argued over what had happened, I just stood there, staring out at the calm blue Nile. *Ali. He couldn't be . . . It couldn't have . . .* I couldn't even whisper to my own mind what might have happened.

A river police boat slowed down near the jetty and I managed to see its occupants. There were two tourists with the police, a man and a woman, wrapped in blankets. I saw that the police were not going to subject them to this crowd and sure enough, their motorboat roared off downstream. Gradually, the crowd grew quieter, some deciding they needed to get on with their daily business. The ferrymen had been as enthralled as everyone else and now they resumed work, and a ferry full to capacity chugged off towards the west bank, allowing another to land and discharge its passengers.

I stood in the middle of the flow of people, bewildered. Eventually I made myself move and ran down to the felucca moorings where surely someone would have seen what happened. There, to my relief, I found two of Ali's friends and fellow felucca captains, Abdou and Nasser. They looked shaken, and were both chain-smoking Cleopatras.

'Is Ali OK?' I asked them. 'What happened? Where is he?'

'We don't know,' Nasser told me. 'Someone say the cruise ship make this problem. Ali ... *yani*, we don't know what happen to him. *Insh'allah* he is OK.'

'*Insh'allah*,' muttered Abdou.

'Nobody see Mahmoud also,' added Nasser. 'Just the tourists.'

A cynical look passed over their faces and I could tell what they were thinking. The priority of the river police and the cruise ship owners would be to take care of the Westerners. They looked at me uncomfortably and returned to discussing it in Arabic, tutting and shaking their heads.

'Maybe another felucca picked them up,' I said desperately. 'Someone must have seen them.'

The two guys appeared not to hear me. I wandered to

the end of the felucca jetty and peered up the river. The waters of the Nile ran smooth and deep, especially out in the middle where the accident must have occurred. I thought of all the times I had lazed in the felucca, trailing my hand in the water. I had never considered the river dangerous. Ali and Mahmoud had always seemed so confident and in control of the little boat and its lofty sail. Now I felt sick to the depths of my stomach.

# Chapter Ten

A felucca was approaching and I stared at its occupants. Others had seen it too, and suddenly I was once more surrounded by men in *galabiyyas*, all shouting and waving to the men in the boat. I craned my neck. The felucca captain was standing on the deck, hollering to everyone, and I saw three figures huddled on the benches. One wore a *galabiyya*. The other two were wrapped in blankets.

'Ali . . .' My throat contracted on the word and my eyes filled with tears. I scarcely dared believe it was him.

Before I could be totally sure, a river police boat scudded up the river and caught up with the felucca. There was a heated exchange between the captain and the police. It was obvious what was going on. The police wanted to take the two survivors away; the captain wanted to bring them to shore himself. And all the while, the figures on the benches were just beyond recognition and I wept with frustration, not caring who could see.

Inevitably, the police won the argument. As if it were not enough that the two had been dunked in the Nile, they were now made to transfer from one boat to the other, mid-stream. As they stood, I got a clearer view and my heart pounded with relief. The shorter one was Mahmoud, clambering into the police boat. The taller one stood with his head bowed, waiting to follow, and I knew it was him. It was Ali.

The men around me were angry. They welcomed the felucca captain ashore along with his assistant and peppered them with questions. I hovered at the fringes, trying to work out what they were saying, but it was hopeless. None of them would talk to me or explain. They were all caught up in their own world and for once it was more important than the attention of a Westerner. I was just in the way.

Feeling lost and empty, I wandered off. I knew that the place to go was Ali's family home, but I couldn't quite face it yet. I just wanted to go somewhere peaceful, which wasn't a readily available option in Luxor. I went back up to the Corniche, then, almost without thinking, I walked along to the entrance to Luxor Temple and paid to get in.

Once I was in, no one bothered me. I found a sunny spot along the avenue of sphinxes and sat down, leaning my back against a solid block of limestone. Tourists were being herded around by guides and I watched them, thinking how weird it was that they had so little idea about the real world around them. They seemed so exposed and vulnerable, at the mercy of the culture they were travelling through. I guess I thought that because right then, despite my inside knowledge, so was I.

The scenes on the riverbank had given me a good idea of what it was going to be like in Ali's home. There would be groups of men sitting around, deep in conversation – relatives and friends of Ali's father. Women wouldn't be included. They'd just serve endless trays of *shai* and keep the children out of the way. And me? I'd be invisible, irrelevant. I'd just have to hope that the police released Ali quickly and that he could get away to talk to me.

I waited an hour, then caught the ferry and a service taxi to the mud-brick house that had become so familiar. And you know, it was exactly as I'd expected, only worse. There was a total sense of crisis. Ali's mother was tearful but she managed to smile at me and usher me through to the main room, where there was an almighty family gathering – every male relative for miles, by the looks of it. Ali's father Ibrahim looked drawn and haggard, his face lined with anxiety, but he nodded an acknowledgement to me as I sat down in one corner. Someone offered me a cigarette, which I refused. Then that was it. They were off, and I didn't hear a word of English for the next hour.

It was hopeless trying to understand. I didn't even bother, though one thing did become clear. Five words kept recurring. *Ali Baba*, which were obvious enough. Felucca, likewise. Then there was *floos*, which I knew meant money, and the final word that I thought I could hear between the others was *beyt*. House. From all this I gathered that the *Ali Baba* had been lost, and that this was the cause for the family conference – not the ordeal that Ali had been through. What the house had to do with it, I wasn't sure.

It was exhausting, sitting there. I wanted to escape but I ached for Ali and I wanted to be there when he returned. At last we heard shouts and a commotion in the courtyard. The door opened. In walked Ali, with Mahmoud just behind.

I felt my stomach flip over. I hadn't realised how badly I needed to see him, or how part of me still barely believed he'd survived. My face split into a smile of relief as he looked around the room and met my gaze.

But I couldn't speak to him. He was pulled into the centre of the room amidst a chorus of *salaams* and *il'hamdu lillahs*, and made to sit next to his father. Everyone wanted to touch him and pat his back, as though he was a returning hero, and his mother brought a fresh round of *shai*. I noticed that Ali raised his glass with trembling fingers and suddenly I felt angry. *I* loved him too, but it was as though I could only view him through a thick glass window. There were questions, questions, endless questions in Arabic and Ali spoke quietly, telling them what had happened. Sometimes he looked across at me and I saw an apology in his eyes – but I also saw exhaustion and a deep, deep anguish.

I began to realise that I wouldn't get to see him on my own that day. His family had closed ranks around him in a crisis that had nothing to do with me. It was dark by now and I decided to leave. As I stood and walked across the room, no one seemed to notice. I turned to look at Ali and he smiled faintly.

'I see you tomorrow, *ya* Jen,' he said.

So he accepted that I was going. Just like that. I couldn't believe he didn't stand up and protest; I thought he'd at least follow me out and speak to me for a few minutes. But I saw the deadness in his eyes and the gaze of the room of men upon me, and I backed away. This wasn't my place. I walked down the road on my own and hailed a service taxi down to the ferry. My heart felt heavy and cold and terribly, horribly alone. Back in the safety of my hotel room, I curled myself around my pillow and cried myself to sleep.

I woke up knowing that something had happened, but for a few moments I couldn't remember what. I got out of bed and opened the shutters in my room to look out on the street below and the blue sky above. Slowly, it all filtered back, and as it did so my heart sank.

I showered and got dressed slowly, trying to think. I

tried to be positive. It couldn't be that bad, I told myself. It had all been so awful yesterday – seeing Ali wet and wrapped in a blanket and carted off by the river police, and then that ghastly gathering. But surely his family would be able to replace the felucca easily enough – there must be insurance and stuff. Then all the hubbub would die down and we'd get back to normal.

Feeling a bit better, I headed over to the west bank, hoping that Ali would be in the *fuul* joint for breakfast as usual. Sure enough, he was sitting there, but not on his own. He was surrounded by guys sitting with him, talking over the events of the day before. The feeling I'd had at Ali's house came flooding back, and suddenly I felt really pissed off. I had a right to talk to Ali too. I took a deep breath and walked in.

'Jen!' Ali's face lit up when he saw me. Which was something, at least.

The guys moved aside to make room for me, and I sat down opposite Ali. 'How are you?' I managed to ask, but then I couldn't stop my anger from rising to the surface. I glared at him. 'We should have talked yesterday.'

'I know this. Sorry, Jen.' Ali looked wretched. He signalled to the other guys and thankfully, they moved away. 'Really, I am very sorry. This bad time for my family.'

'But you could have spoken to me.' I knew it was unreasonable, but this was bad time for me too.

Ali didn't have an answer. He shrugged helplessly. '*Yani*, you see my family yesterday. Everybody come and talk and want to know what happen with the felucca . . . also the river police, they ask me question, question, they want to see paper for the felucca and what I say? The paper is finish. The paper in the Nile with *Ali Baba*.'

I frowned. 'What do you mean? The paper's in the Nile?'

'Jen, you know what happen to *Ali Baba*.' Ali seemed agitated and angry, and I could feel my own temper rising too.

'As a matter of fact, Ali, no,' I snapped. 'I don't know. I don't know anything because nobody has bothered to tell me. I don't speak Arabic, remember?'

Ali stared at me, wide-eyed. 'Nobody tell you?' he repeated.

I shook my head, and as distress spread across Ali's face I realised that we were both desperately upset, but thankfully not with each other.

'Jen, I sorry,' said Ali, his eyes beseeching me to understand.

'I was so worried,' I whispered. 'I thought you'd drowned. And then, afterwards, it was just like I didn't exist. No one would talk to me . . .' I bit my lip, not wanting to cry in the café again. Those guys would think I was a permanent tap.

Ali reached for my hand. 'Listen. I talk to you now.'

I squeezed his fingers and nodded. 'So what were you

saying about the felucca? About the papers?'

Ali's face clouded over. He sighed and tutted. 'The river police make big problem with me because I not have papers. I say to them, the papers in the felucca and the felucca in the Nile.'

I didn't fully understand. 'What kind of papers?' I asked. 'You mean your licence?'

Ali nodded. He ran a hand through his hair. '*Yani*, what I do now, *ya* Jen? How I make money?'

I gaped at him. 'You'll get another felucca, won't you?'

Ali gave a cracked laugh. 'And how I buy new felucca? I pray to Allah?'

'But . . . there must be insurance.'

'What this . . . inshu . . .'

I didn't know the Arabic for insurance and I couldn't seem to make him understand. I gathered that whatever system there was, it wasn't as simple as in the UK and anyway, it turned out that the captain of the cruise ship blamed Ali for the accident. I worked out from Ali's description that he had been tacking towards the east shore when the ship had pulled out from the bank, and he didn't have time to get out of the way.

'I think he not look,' said Ali. 'He not see me. How he not see big felucca like *Ali Baba*? *Ya salaam!*' He hit his forehead with his hand in disbelief.

It also turned out that Ali's father had spent all the family savings on the new house that was under construction – the house that would, one day, be Ali's marital home. So that was why I'd kept on hearing the word for house. As Ali talked, I began to get more and more confused. He didn't know most of the words for what he was trying to say and there seemed to be so many if and buts that I couldn't make sense of what was happening.

One thing was clear enough: there was no way of buying a felucca right now. There simply wasn't any money. Relatives might lend some, but no one had actually volunteered it. And it seemed that there was now a problem over Ali's licence. I couldn't work out whether that was because it had gone down with the boat or because the cruise ship had blamed him for the accident. I couldn't work out what other papers there were at all, let alone insurance papers, and it was obviously all a bureaucratic nightmare in any case.

Ali finished talking and we lapsed into silence. I picked at a ball of *taamiya*, half-heartedly. I felt numb. I couldn't believe everything had changed, just like that, overnight. But somehow it had. Ali's face said it all. He could think about nothing else – what he was going to do, how they were going to survive. Above all, he seemed worried about his father and whether he would ever forgive him.

'It wasn't your fault,' I said softly. 'It was an accident.'

Ali looked distraught. 'But this the boat of my father. He buy this when he is very small and he never make accident in all his life.'

'Ali, surely he's not going to blame you?'

Miserably, Ali played with the mashed *fuul*, turning it over with his fork. '*Yani*, I don't know. I worry now how I pay his medicine. And how he finish the house.'

It dawned on me then just how much Ali's life was wrapped up with his family. Of course, I'd known it before, but now I saw that it was *everything*. He had followed in his father's footsteps, captained his father's boat. And the house was being built bang next door to the old one on land that had been in the family for centuries. That was where Ali expected to live when he married. My insides curled. If I stayed, that was where I'd live too.

I didn't know what to say. My hand fingered the *ankh* around my neck: the symbol of life. It seemed incredible that it was only yesterday that Ali had given it to me. 'You're still alive, Ali,' I said eventually. 'That's the most important thing. You could have been killed.'

It seemed to help. Ali looked solemn. 'This true,' he agreed. 'Me, Mahmoud, and the tourists also. *Il'hamdu lillah*, we are safe.'

He pushed his food to one side and so did I. We'd barely touched it.

'I go to my father now,' said Ali. 'I talk with him and with my uncles. *Ya* Jen, you come later, to my house?'

He must have seen the hesitation in my eyes. I wasn't sure I could handle another session like the one the day before.

'Not like yesterday,' he reassured me. 'Not so many people. I sit with you. We eat.'

I took a deep breath. 'OK,' I agreed. 'I'll come and find you later.'

I went back over the river, staring down from the ferry deck. The water swirled beneath me, deep and murky. I shivered, and thought of the *Ali Baba* lying in its grave. It wasn't a pleasant thought.

I didn't want to be on my own, so I decided to hunt out Tina to while away the day. I found her writing in her notebook in our favourite café.

'Hey,' she said warmly, as I walked up to her. 'I heard what happened. The guys on the Corniche told me – well, roughly, anyway. Is everything OK?'

I sat down and ordered a *kerkedi*. 'Not really,' I said.

Tina looked concerned. I told her the whole story, as far as I'd been able to work it out myself. She listened intently, then let out a long, slow breath.

'He was lucky,' she said. 'Really lucky. They all were. There was a tragic accident a few years back in a motor-boat. Can't remember exactly what happened but several people drowned. They dredged the river for days but the currents here are so strong and the riverbed's a mass of weeds. Some of the bodies were never found.'

It wasn't much comfort. I told her that Ali didn't seem to think he'd be able to buy a new felucca, and that didn't surprise her either.

'People aren't insured up to the hilt the way they are in

Britain,' she said. 'Once something's gone, it's gone. Of course there are regulations but it's all so arbitrary. The river police are officious bastards – they'll zoom up and down the river checking the captains' licences and whether the feluccas have fire extinguishers, but have you ever seen anyone wearing a life jacket?'

It was true. I'd never even thought about it before.

'Fire extinguishers!' snorted Tina, shaking her head. Then she sighed. 'It'll all change in time, of course. Well, it might. Who knows?'

I decided I didn't want to talk about it any more. Another worry was niggling away at me and I had to broach it. If Ali had no income, I was going to have to find one sooner rather than later.

'Did you manage to speak to anyone about work?' I asked her. 'Something tells me I'm going to need it.'

Tina looked uncomfortable. 'I asked around,' she said vaguely. 'I'm afraid I didn't come up with anything. The hotels tend to employ locals, and to be a guide you really need to know your Egyptology. Can you teach?'

'Teach what?'

'English.'

'Well . . . I haven't before or anything. I haven't had any training.' To be honest, the mere idea scared me witless – especially here.

'It might be your best bet,' said Tina. 'But if you don't have a qualification you'd have to work for some kind of unofficial school. I've heard of them in Cairo, I'm not sure about here. You could ask around.'

I felt panic rising. 'I wouldn't know where to start,' I said.

Tina looked sympathetic. 'I know what you mean. It's not easy here, Jen. And the longer you spend here, the more unfathomable it all seems.' She hesitated, then leaned over towards me. 'You know, there's nothing wrong with admitting that something's too difficult. Nothing wrong at all.'

I couldn't bear it. Not right then. I buried my face in my hands. 'Don't say that,' I begged, through my fingers. 'I have to stay. Somehow, I have to work it out. Can't you see that?' I took my hands away and gazed at her.

'What I see . . .' began Tina, then stopped. She thought for a moment. 'What I see is someone trying very hard, against the odds. That's all. And that's OK, because the most important thing that anyone can say about their life is that they've tried.'

There was something so tired and sad in her voice, and suddenly I realised that she must have tried at something here too. And I guessed that she had failed. Here she was, on her own, a woman older than my mum, just passing time. *Seen it all, done it all, got the T-shirt*, that's what she'd said. I looked up and saw there were tears in her eyes and I felt mine fill up too.

We caught sight of each other's distress and in seconds,

we were both rummaging for tissues. 'Oh, Tina,' I wept, reaching for her hand across the table. 'I'm so glad I met you here. I don't know what I would have done . . .'

She reached out and squeezed my fingers as we both managed to pull ourselves together. Then she dabbed at her eyes and gave me a teary grin. 'Well, don't count on me sticking around,' she said, 'and I've a feeling I shouldn't count on you either.'

I tried not to hear the second part of the sentence. Instead, I blew my nose and called the waiter over. '*Min fadlak*,' I said in my best Arabic. '*Momkin kerkedi tani?*' Another *kerkedi*, please.


As Ali had promised, most of the relatives and friends had disappeared by the time I arrived at his family home in the mid-afternoon. All the same, there was tension in the air. His uncle Tayib was sitting with Ibrahim, along with another uncle I recognised from yesterday's gathering.

Ali greeted me and I sat down. I smiled and went through the usual ritual of refusing everyone's offer of cigarettes. His mother appeared in the doorway and I accepted the offer of *shai*. The men were quiet. If anything, Ibrahim looked even more haggard than he had the day before, and his persistent hacking cough seemed to have got worse.

Ali was preoccupied and studied his fingernails while we waited for the *shai*. Somehow I sensed that he was angry, and nervous. He sat close to me, as he had said he would – closer than he usually did when I was in the family home.

Tayib said something to him in Arabic and he responded tersely. Ibrahim chipped in with something else, and then there was a brief, heated exchange between all four of them.

Ali inched slightly closer to me, protectively, and I suddenly twigged. They were talking about *me*. The three older men were staring right at me, their gaze angry and accusatory.

'What's going on?' I asked, looking around. 'Ali, what are you all saying?'

Ali's expression was furious. 'Nothing,' he said.

Tayib exclaimed to him angrily and they all started off again. I listened carefully, trying to pick up clues. When I heard the word *floos*, I got it. Oh, I got it all right. They thought I was loaded, and they were trying to get Ali to ask me for money. It was as clear as the morning air.

'I don't have any money!' I burst out, before I could stop myself. I glared at them. 'I only have enough for a few months. After that I've got nothing. My family don't want me to be here so if you think I'm rich, you can forget it.'

There was a shocked silence. I wasn't sure if the second uncle spoke English but I knew that Tayib and Ibrahim understood perfectly. In fact, they looked embarrassed.

'*Ya* Jen, *ya* Jen,' said Ibrahim, shaking his head. 'We don't

want your money.' He smiled apologetically as Hasina
arrived with the *shai*. 'Just we make talk. Not more.'

Hasina handed round the glasses of *shai*. I reached for
mine with trembling fingers. I didn't believe Ali's father
but I knew he was trying to save face; the fact that I'd
understood had shamed them all.

Gently, subtly, I felt Ali's knee make contact with mine,
and I wished I could fling my arms around him and bury
my head in his shoulder. Instead, I blew on my *shai*.

Shortly afterwards, the uncles left. The rest of the
afternoon and evening passed awkwardly, but there was
no more talk of money or the felucca. We sat down to eat.
Now, the whole family ate together around a big platter on
the floor whenever I visited, not just the men. I realised it
meant that I was no longer a guest – I was accepted as one
of them. As Tayib had said when I arrived, I was *family*.
But after everything that had happened, I didn't find it
much of a comfort.

Everyone was quiet as we shared the food. I could see
that Ali's mother was still upset and anxious. I wondered
how much she knew of what went on; pretty much all of
it, I guessed. She'd have her say. Gradually, I'd come to see
that the family was much closer than it had first appeared.
Ibrahim relied on her a lot. In fact, everyone relied on
everyone else – the men, the women, the children, as well
as the uncles, cousins and aunts.

I didn't know where I fitted in, though, or if I ever

could. How would I find it, living for real in this claustrophobic culture? My heart felt like lead. Ali kept throwing me little sidelong glances and part of me longed to be alone with him. Another part just longed to be alone.

I thought long and hard that night, tossing and turning under the sheet. There was an answer to everything at the edge of my mind but I didn't want to have to face it. All I could think was how much I loved Ali and how I couldn't bear what had happened. There had to be a way. There *had* to be a way. But however hard I thought, there was only that little niggling answer sitting there, weeping, at the edge of my mind.

By dawn I felt shattered, in more ways than one. I got up, showered and dressed, and headed quietly out of the hotel. Everything I saw was like the twist of a knife in my heart. The dozing caleche horses, munching their fodder. The morning light on Luxor temple. The old women walking along the streets dressed head to toe in black, their faces wrinkled. A black kite hovering above the Corniche, its forked tail bending to the wind. And my favourite sight of all: morning sun on the golden-pink mountains of the west bank with their secret treasury of tombs, and the fresh reflected blue of the sky on the waters of the Nile.

I didn't go to meet Ali for breakfast as I usually did. I went instead to the Pharaoh's stables and hired my favourite horse. The guys there knew me now, and trusted me to take the mare out on my own. I rode her along all my favourite routes: through the farmland and down towards the river, where the reedbeds twittered and chattered with birds, back up through the little mud-brick villages, where villagers viewed me with idle curiosity as I clattered through and children chased half-heartedly behind me and chickens squawked and fluttered out of the way. Then I followed a little irrigation channel to what the locals called the *moroor*, the traffic junction, and headed west, out to where the fields of wheat and sugarcane stretched to reach the mountains and the desert.

Here, I eased the reins and let my mare go. We cantered along the dusty tracks and out beyond, crossing the little tram-lines that were used to transport the crops of sugarcane. More villages, donkeys and buffalos, and the morning call of laughing doves in the stillness.

We reached the desert fringe, where a rough line of dunes formed a barrier between the farmland and the endless miles of stones and rocks that lay beyond. The horses loved to gallop through the tough mounds of sand to the top, so up we went. Here, there was often a hot wind blowing in from the desert, but the morning air was still. I dismounted, patted my faithful mare, and stared into the distance.

This was what I'd seen, on that first fateful flight into Luxor. The place where the fertile land turns to desert. The place where plants cease to grow. A strange, alien land belonging to people with strange, alien ways. I hadn't been wrong, back then. This place was special, and so were its people. I'd had a magical, wonderful time . . . and as I realised I was already thinking in the past tense I felt my stomach heave. I leaned my head against my mare's neck for a moment, tears blurring my eyes. She looked round at me mildly, her delicate ears pricked. I hugged her, and let myself cry.

I stayed there for a long time, thinking, and yet trying not to think. I knew that something had shifted deep inside me that I could barely put into words, even in my own mind. But it was something about who I really was, and where I really belonged.

Eventually, I remounted and rode slowly back, via the ancient temple of Medinet Habu. I reined my mare in to gaze at this view; it was always awesome. Through the grand mud-brick walls were glimpses of the wonderful stone temple within, and the mountains rose majestically behind. I remembered how it had felt when I had explored the Valley of the Kings with Karen, Mar and Izzy – the valley that was hidden within those mountain walls. It seemed a century ago.

Ali had waited for me at the *fuul* joint for over an hour. But someone, of course, had seen me riding out – nothing was ever a secret here! – and had passed the news on to him. He came to meet me as I walked slowly from the stables to the ferry.

We both stopped when we saw each other. Just stopped, yards apart, and looked. My heart was yammering painfully in my chest, and I felt I could hardly breathe. Just from the way he stood, his shoulders hunched, I knew he knew. We both knew: the fact was, everything had changed. I thought my heart would break. Wasn't love strong enough for anything? Wasn't that what everyone was supposed to believe? And in a flash I heard my mum's voice in my head. *Sometimes it is. Sometimes it isn't.* A voice from my own world, the world I'd been so sure I wanted to leave.

'Jen.'

The spell was broken, and I walked up to him, a fixed, sad smile on my lips.

'Sorry I didn't come . . .' I began.

Ali shook his head. 'This not matter.'

He told me how he'd found out where I was, and then we walked to the ferry as though nothing had happened. I almost asked him if he was going out in the felucca later on, but stopped myself in time. Instead, I told him I needed to send some e-mails, and agreed to meet him later. Our fingers touched, our eyes met, and I was reminded how much we loved each other. And then I stepped away from him, on to the ferry.

I needed to let it all out. I wrote to Karen, and now I

found the words that I hadn't been able to whisper to myself out on my ride. This wasn't about Ali. I knew I still loved him, and that I always would. It was everything else. It was being an outsider in a tight-knit family in which everyone knew each other's business and women served the *shai*. It was trying to find a voice in a world I'd never fully understand. If I was going to fit in – and I wasn't sure I ever could – I'd have to forget the person I'd fought to become. I'd battled day in, day out with my dad for the freedom to be myself, and now I knew I couldn't give that up. Not for this. Not for the life I'd have here.

I felt my heart was going to burst with love and sadness, but I knew what I had to do. And I knew I couldn't tell Ali. I had four days left before my return flight – the flight I never thought I would take. And in those four days I loved him with my whole heart. I saw how lost he was, without a felucca. *Felucca is all I know.* I saw how his family needed him. And I saw what a good, beautiful man he was and how he did not deserve his misfortune.

I went to the bank and changed the rest of Aunt Carrie's money to Egyptian pounds. All of it. I reckoned it would pay for a felucca. Oh, I thought about it long and hard, of course. I thought about the uncles and Ibrahim and the way they thought of me; about the two houses and the comparative poverty of doctors. But somehow it wasn't the point. I was doing this for Ali, as the only way I knew to show I loved him. He might not believe it at first. He'd be angry that I had abandoned him. He might even think I was like all the others. But I hoped – God, I hoped! – that in time he'd see the truth, and forgive me.

I had to plan my last day carefully. I knew that Ali wouldn't accept the money. And I knew that if we talked about it, I'd change my mind about going in any case. So I waited until the last minute. I packed and I arranged for a taxi to take me to the airport. Only then did I go and find him.

He was sitting in the courtyard of his family home, smoking. I crouched down next to him and stroked his hand. He smiled absently and played with my fingers, his mind far away. I rested my head on his shoulder for a moment. Then I handed him the envelope. A big, brown envelope.

'What this, *ya* Jen?' he asked, startled.

'Don't look now,' I whispered. 'Please don't look now.'

Ali did as I said. Instead, he looked at me. I don't know how long we sat, drinking each other in. We both knew what was happening but neither of us could bring ourselves to say it. At last, I had to tear myself away.

I stood. '*Maa'salaama*, *ya* Ali,' I said softly. '*Ana behebak.*'

Goodbye, Ali. I love you.

He still looked at me, his eyes full of sorrow and

understanding. I saw him swallow. '*Maa'salaama, habibi,*' he whispered back.

I stood up, and walked away, then turned to see his face one last time. Ali's eyes were closed, his cheeks streaked with tears. I couldn't speak. I couldn't cry either. I just raised my hand, even though he wasn't looking, and left the courtyard.

My time to cry came later. As the plane rose into the sky and I looked down at the desert, I could barely see it for tears. I fingered the *ankh* around my neck, but I knew that Ali had given me something far more precious than that. He had shown me another life and invited me openly to join it. I knew I would never forget his love and the beauty of what we had shared. And as the plane rose and the desert became a distant sheet of yellow, I remembered what Tina had said. *The most important thing that anyone can say about their life is that they tried.*

And I knew, with all my heart, that we had tried.

# Acknowledgements

This book wouldn't have been written if Brenda Gardner at Piccadilly and my agent Rosemary Canter hadn't believed in it, so I owe my biggest thanks to them. Thanks to the rest of the Piccadilly team too, especially Yasemin for her sterling editing. I would also like to acknowledge Jessica, Helen, Adele and Gemma for their insights into student life, Hannah and Kate for their holiday memories, Katherine for her wise comments on the first draft, and Arielle, Laura and Becky at Sheffield Uni, who were clearly having a much better time than Jen.